# THE CRESSET LIBRARY

GENERAL EDITOR: JOHN HAYWARD

A

# ON THE EVE

# Ivan Sergeevich Turgenev

# ON THE EVE

Translated from the Russian by
MOURA BUDBERG

LONDON
THE CRESSET PRESS
MCML

*First published in* 1950
*by The Cresset Press Ltd.,* 11 *Fitzroy Square, London W.*1,
*and printed in Great Britain at*
*The Chiswick Press, New Southgate, London, N.*11

# EDITORIAL NOTE

ON THE EVE, the third of Turgenev's novels in order of publication, originally appeared in 1859 as a serial in *The Russian Herald* and was issued as a book in the same year. Although it had been preceded chronologically by *Rudin* (1855) and *A House of Gentlefolk* (1858), the idea of it had been conceived while Turgenev was working at his first novel. "At that time," he afterwards recalled, "various ideas were swarming in my head. I wanted to settle down to write *Rudin*, but the theme I was trying to develop in *On the Eve* intermittently obtruded itself. I could imagine quite clearly the character of the heroine, Elena . . . but I had no hero, no one to whom with her vague but powerful yearning for freedom she could abandon herself."

It was during this difficult stage in his work, while he was living on the family estate at Spaskoye, that he read again the small manuscript notebook which Vassili Karatiev, a friend and neighbour, had given him before leaving for the Crimean War. In it Karatiev had briefly recorded the story of his unhappy love-affair with a Moscow girl who had jilted him in favour of a Bulgarian named Katranov. Karatiev (who was to die of typhus in the Crimea) had expressed a wish that in the event of his death Turgenev should make what use he could of the story.

This chance rereading of it was to provide, in the person of Katranov, the hero Turgenev had been looking for. In so far as Katranov is the Insarov of the novel (dying as he did of phthisis in Venice on his way home to Bulgaria), and Karatiev himself an adumbration of Shubin; in so far again as a visit to the Tsaritsin Lakes is a crucial incident in both, Karatiev's story is, in outline, the story of *On the Eve*. But it is no more than this, and Turgenev could not have turned his friend's jejune narrative into a masterpiece merely by filling in the outline. *On the Eve* is indeed a striking example of the power of imagination to transmute plain facts into a work of art.

Karatiev's experience gave Turgenev the prototype of the hero he needed for Elena; but it gave him also a situation in which he could exercise his ironic humour and his delicate compassion. For, although it was in fact a simple, even commonplace experience, it contained those two conflicting elements—purity and self-surrender of first love and ardour and selflessness of revolutionary action—the combination of which (always a fascinating problem to Turgenev) he was to achieve with complete success in the idyll of Insarov and Elena. The first moved him to the compassionate tenderness which he shows for all his heroines in love, and for Elena more than for any of them; the second to the irony, softened by a smile, which he employed to disguise his disbelief in the possibility of social and political reform in the Russia of his day. Although, as a sceptic, he was to deny his hero the fruits of action—Insarov, like Bazarov in *Fathers and Children*, was to die "on the eve"—the sense of disenchantment, which suffuses the whole novel with a saddening autumnal mood, is mitigated by the springlike freshness and promise of Elena's love. Turgenev, a romantic at heart, created in Elena, the most affecting and the most admirable of his heroines, one who in her fearless surrender to her destiny was immune from his irony.

An unconscious tribute to Turgenev's power of characterization was paid by his contemporaries who discussed Elena and Insarov as if they were actual people, arguing about the unconventionality of the one and the patriotic motives of the other as if both were capable of subverting Russian society. It is not surprising that they reacted thus, for the historical background of the novel was real to its early readers. The Crimean War had ended only three years before *On the Eve* was published and the "incidents" which had precipitated it and to which Turgenev incidentally refers—the occupation by the Russians of the "Principalities" of Wallachia and Moldavia; the Turkish ultimatum; the "Massacre of Sinope"—were fresh in their memory.

Behind the Iron Curtain, which has since fallen between Russia and the West, it may be that the political and sociological aspects of *On the Eve* are still discussed; but to Turgenev's English readers they will appear dim and remote in the shadows cast by the light that illuminates the two principal actors. For *On the Eve* is primarily a tale of two lovers and it is as foils to them that all the other characters—Elena's absurd father and hypochondriacal mother; the young sculptor and the student of philosophy; the pompous civil servant and the German flirt; and "uncle" Uvar, the most lovable of all Turgenev's wise fools—have a part in the drama of their meeting and union and final separation by death.

J. H.

A*

# ACKNOWLEDGMENT

*I wish to express my deep gratitude to Mr. John Hayward, the General Editor of the series in which this translation appears, for his encouragement, criticism and help at every stage.*

M. B.

# ON THE EVE

## CHAPTER I

ON ONE OF the hottest summer days of 1853, in the shade of a tall lime tree on the bank of the river Moskva, not far from Kunzovo, two young men lay stretched out on the grass. One of them, about twenty-three years old, tall and swarthy, with a sharp and slightly crooked nose, a high forehead and a restrained smile on his broad lips, lay on his back and gazed dreamily into the distance, his small grey eyes half-closed; the other lay on his chest, propping up his fair, curly head with both hands, also staring into space. He was three years older than his friend, but looked much younger: the moustache on his upper lip hardly showed and there was light curly down on his chin. There was something childishly attractive, appealing and graceful in the small features of his fresh round face, in the melting brown eyes, the well-shaped pouting lips and white hands. He exuded the happy light-heartedness that goes with health and youth—a care-free, self-assured, self-indulgent, winsome youth. The play of his eyes, his smile, the manner in which he propped up his head—his whole behaviour was that of a boy accustomed to attract admiration. He wore a loose white coat, like an overall, a blue cravat was tied round his slender neck, a crumpled straw hat was flung on the grass near by.

By comparison, his companion seemed an old man, and watching his gawky appearance, no one would have guessed that he, too, was enjoying the moment, that he, too, was content. He lay in an uncomfortable attitude; his head, wide at the top and narrow at the base, sat awkwardly on his long neck; the very position of his arms and of his body, which was tightly squeezed into a short black coat, and of his long legs with their knees raised like the hind legs of a grasshopper, made him look uncomfortable. It was impossible, however, to mistake him for anything but a well-educated young man; for all his ungainliness the stamp of "good breeding" was there, and his face, ugly and even slightly comical, was kind and not without a thoughtful quality. His name was Andrei Petrovich Bersenev; his companion, the fair-haired young man, was called Pavel Jakovlevich Shubin.

"Why don't you lie on your chest like me?" Shubin asked; "it's much better that way. Particularly if you lift your legs up and knock one heel against the other—like this. You've got the grass under your nose, and if you get tired of watching the scenery, you can look at a pot-bellied insect climbing up a stalk, or an ant fussing around. It's really much more fun this way. Now you—you've adopted a kind of pseudo-classical pose—a perfect imitation of a ballet dancer leaning against a cardboard rock. Try to remember that you're fully entitled to a rest—it's no joke passing out third from the top in one's finals. Relax, sir, stretch your legs, rest on your oars."

Shubin delivered this speech half-jokingly, with a lazy

drawl (spoilt children speak like this to old friends of the family, who bring them sweets) and went on without waiting for a reply.

"What surprises me most in ants, beetles and other worthy insects is their remarkable earnestness: they rush to and fro in such a solemn way—as if their lives were of the faintest importance! Why, here is Man, the Lord of Creation, the superior being, gazing at them, and they take no notice of him. What's more, one of these mosquitoes might at any moment sit on the Lord of Creation's nose and make use of it for purposes of nourishment. It's monstrous. On the other hand, is their life any worse than ours? And why shouldn't they feel important if we allow ourselves that luxury? Eh, you over there, you're a philosopher, can't you solve this problem? Have you nothing to say about it?"

"What is it?" Bersenev murmured with a start.

"What?" repeated Shubin. "Here's your friend communicating his profound ideas to you and you don't even listen to him."

"I was admiring the view. Look how those fields glow in the sun!" (Bersenev had a slight lisp.)

"Yes, a fine splash of colour, no doubt," muttered Shubin. "Nature, in a word."

Bersenev shook his head. "As an artist *you* ought to be the one to marvel at it. It's in your line."

"Excuse me, it's not in my line at all," protested Shubin, putting his hat on the back of his head. "I'm a butcher, if you please; my line is flesh, modelling flesh—shoulders, arms and legs; there's no form here, no finish— it sprawls all over the place, there's no holding it."

3

"But there's beauty in it, all the same," remarked Bersenev. "By the way, have you finished your bas-relief?"

"Which one?"

"The child with the goat."

"To hell with it! To hell!" Shubin exclaimed in a singsong tone. "I took a look at the real thing, at the old masters, and smashed my bit of rubbish to pieces. You point at the view and say, 'There's beauty in it, all the same.' Of course, there's beauty in everything, beauty even in your nose, but one can't be chasing it all the time. The old masters didn't even try to. It descended on their works of its own accord, heaven knows from where— from the sky, probably. The whole world belonged to them; we can't allow ourselves all that room, our arms are too short. All we can do is cast our line at one little spot and keep watch. It's grand if it bites, but if it doesn't . . . ." Shubin put out his tongue.

"Wait a bit, wait," said Bersenev. "You're being paradoxical. If you don't have a sense of beauty and don't love it wherever you find it, why, then, you won't find it in your art. If a beautiful view or beautiful music means nothing to you, that is if you don't harmonize. . . ."

"Ah, you old harmonizer," broke in Shubin, who was the first to laugh at the newly-coined word, while Bersenev became buried in thought. "No, my boy," Shubin continued, "you're a distinguished philosopher, third graduate at Moscow University, it's dangerous to argue with you, especially for me, the half-baked student, but I must tell you this all the same: that, apart from my particular branch of art, I only love beauty in women, in girls, and that only lately. . . ."

He turned over on his back and folded his arms under

his head. A few moments passed in silence. The stillness of the blazing noonday lay heavily over the radiant and drowsy countryside.

"Talking of women," Shubin went on, "why doesn't somebody do something about Stakhov? Did you see him in Moscow?"

"No."

"The old fellow has quite gone off his head. He sits day after day with his Augustina Khristianovna, terribly bored, but he goes on sitting all the same. They just stare at each other, it's too idiotic. Disgusting to watch in fact. Now, how do you explain that? What a family the good Lord has blessed him with! But no, he must have his Augustina Khristianovna! I've never seen anything more distasteful than her duck's profile. I modelled a caricature of her the other day in the style of Dantan*—not bad at all. I'll show it to you."

"And the bust of Elena Nikolaevna?" inquired Bersenev, "Is that progressing?"

"No, my boy, not at all. Her face is enough to drive anyone to despair. At first sight you think it's easy to get a likeness—such pure, straight, severe lines. Nothing of the kind. You can't get it just by holding out your hand for it. Have you ever noticed the way she listens? Not a tremor on her features, only a constant change of expression which alters the whole appearance. What is a sculptor to do, and a bad one at that? A wonderful person . . . a strange person," he added, after a short silence.

"Yes, she's a wonderful girl," Bersenev repeated.

"And she's the daughter of Nikolai Artemievich

* Jean Pierre Dantan, French satirical sculptor, 1800-1869.—
*Translator's note.*

5

Stakhov. What's one to say about blood and race after that? Yet the funny thing is she's very much his daughter, she's like him, and she's also like her mother, Anna Vassilievna. I'm very fond of Anna Vassilievna; she's my benefactress, but she's an old hen, all the same. Where does Elena get that spiritual quality from, then? Who struck that spark in her? There's another problem for you, philosopher.''

But the ''philosopher'', as usual, was silent. In any case Bersenev was not the talkative sort and, when he did speak, expressed himself clumsily, stammered, and gesticulated. And at that particular moment a peculiar stillness had come over him, a stillness akin to lassitude, to sadness. He had only recently moved out of town after a long and tedious job which had taken up many hours of his time every day. Idleness, languor, the limpid air, the satisfaction of an aim achieved, a casual and whimsical conversation with a friend, the sudden evocation of someone dear to him—all these diverse and, at the same time, strangely analogous experiences, were blended into a single sensation which soothed, excited, and debilitated him—all at the same time. He was somewhat highly strung.

It was cool and peaceful under the lime-tree. The flies and bees that came flying into the circle of its shade seemed to hum more softly; the short grass, fresh and emerald-coloured, without a tinge of gold in it, did not stir, its upright blades standing motionless, as if spellbound; the little clusters of yellow flowers on the lower branches of the lime-tree were still as death. Their sweet smell penetrated with every breath to the very depths of the lungs, and how willingly the lungs inhaled it. In the distance, beyond the river, everything blazed and glowed as far as the eye could see; from time to time a breeze passed over and enhanced the glow by its disturbance. A shimmering vapour drifted over the earth. The birds were silent—they stop singing during the sultry hours of the day; but the grasshoppers were chattering everywhere, and it was pleasant to hear this fervent hum of life in the restful coolness. It sent one off to sleep and encouraged dreaming.

"Have you ever noticed," Bersenev suddenly began, underlining his argument with the play of his hands, "what strange feelings Nature produces in us? Everything about her is so clear and complete—I mean, so satisfied with itself; we understand and admire her and at the same time she arouses—anyway, she does in me—a feeling of anxiety, restlessness, even sadness. Why should she do this? Is it because when we confront her we are more keenly aware of our inadequacy and ambiguity; or is it because we need something more than that complacency which seems to satisfy her, and she has nothing more to give us—that is to say, she can't give us what we really want?"

"Hm . . . ," Shubin replied. "I'll tell you, Andrei Petrovich, what it all comes from. You have just described the feelings of a lonely man, who is not really alive, but just a feeble looker-on. What is there to look at? Just try to live and you'll be all right. You may knock as much as you like at Nature's door, but she won't give you an intelligible answer, because she can't speak. Nature may twang and reverberate like a string, only you mustn't expect a song from her. But the human heart will answer you, especially a woman's heart. And so, my noble friend, my advice to you is to get yourself a sweetheart and all your dreary yearnings will instantly vanish. That is what we "want" —to use your word. All this sorrow and anguish is, after

7

all, nothing more than a kind of hunger. Give your stomach its proper food and everything will come right. Give your body a place in the world, my boy. What's all this nonsense about Nature? Listen to the sound of the word *love*; what strength and fire there is in it! *Nature*—what a cold, pedantic word. And so . . .", Shubin lilted, " . . . 'Long live Maria Petrovna' . . .! No," he added, "not Maria Petrovna, but it's all the same. Vous me comprenez."

Bersenev raised himself and rested his chin on his folded arms.

"Why the mockery?" he murmured without glancing at his friend, "Why the banter? You're right, love is a great word, a great emotion. . . . But what sort of love have you in mind?"

Shubin raised himself, too. "What sort of love? Any sort, as long as it's there. To tell you the truth, I don't believe there are different sorts of love. Once you're in love. . . ."

"With all your soul," added Bersenev.

"Well, of course, one takes that for granted. The soul's not an apple, it can't be divided. Once you're in love, you're doing the right thing, and I wasn't mocking at all. There's such a feeling of tenderness in my heart now, such serenity. . . . All I wanted was to explain why you think Nature has this effect on us. Because she awakens in us the desire of love and is incapable of satisfying it. She gently pushes us into another and a warmer embrace, and, failing to understand the gesture, we expect something from Nature herself. Ah, Andrei, Andrei, look how beautiful the sun is, and the sky; everything around us is beautiful. Yet you're sad. But if at this moment you were holding in your hand the hand of the woman you love, if the hand and

8

the woman belonged to you, if you were seeing with her eyes and feeling, not with the feelings of a lonely man, but with hers, it wouldn't be sadness or anguish, Andrei, that Nature would rouse in you and you wouldn't be thinking of Nature's beauty; Nature herself would be filled with joy and sing and echo your exaltation, because you would have given a tongue to her dumbness.''

Shubin jumped to his feet and walked twice up and down, while Bersenev lowered his face which had become slightly flushed.

"I don't quite agree with you," he began, "Nature doesn't always conjure up . . . love." (He hesitated before uttering this word.) "She also threatens us, reminds us of terrifying . . . yes, of mysteries beyond our reach. Isn't she going to absorb us one day, isn't she continually doing so? Life and Death are both involved in her and the voice of Death is just as loud as Life's."

Shubin interrupted him: "Love, too, is both Life and Death."

"Besides," continued Bersenev, "when I stand, for instance, in the forest on a spring morning, in a green clearing and imagine I hear the romantic sound of Oberon's horn . . ." (Bersenev looked embarrassed as he pronounced these words) " . . . Is that, too. . . ."

"The yearning for love, the yearning for happiness— nothing more," observed Shubin. "I, too, know these sounds, I know the expectancy and emotion that overcome one in the depth of the forest, in its shade; or in an open field in the evening, when the sun is setting and the mist rises from the river behind the bushes. But it is happiness I'm waiting for—from the forest, the river, the earth and the sky, from every little cloud and every blade of grass.

It's happiness I want; I feel it coming, I hear it calling to me! 'Oh God, my bright and happy God!' I once began a poem like that. It's a good first line, you'll agree, but I couldn't think of another one. Yes, happiness, before life passes us by, while we have control of our limbs, while we go up, not downhill. Hang it all!'' Shubin burst out suddenly, "We're young, we're not monsters, or idiots; we'll achieve our happiness!''

He shook out his curls and glanced up at the sky, full of self-assurance, almost defiantly. Bersenev looked up at him. 'Is there then nothing more important than happiness?'' he murmured softly.

"What, for instance?'' asked Shubin, and stopped.

"Well, for instance, you and I, as you say, are young. Let's admit we're good. Let's say we each want happiness for ourselves. But would this word happiness unite us, light a mutual flame in us, make us clasp each other's hands warmly? Isn't it an egotistical word, I mean, a disuniting one?''

"Do you know the ones that unite?''

"Yes, I do. There are quite a lot of them and you know them, too.''

"What are they?''

"Well, why not art—as you're an artist—or one's country, or science, or freedom, or justice?''

"And love?'' asked Shubin.

"Love, too, is a uniting word, but not the love you're now so excited about, not ecstatic love, but altruistic love.''

Shubin frowned. "That's all right for the Germans. I want love for my own sake. I want to come first.''

"Come first?'' repeated Bersenev. "In my opinion, to take second place is one's mission in life.''

"If everybody behaved according to your advice," Shubin muttered, putting on a plaintive look, "nobody in the world would eat pineapples; they'd always pass them on to someone else."

"Which means that pineapples aren't really necessary. Besides, you need have no fear, there'll always be someone ready to snatch even bread from the other man's mouth."

The two friends remained silent for a time.

"I met Insarov again the other day," began Bersenev; "I asked him to come and see me. I do want you and the Stakhovs to get to know him."

"Who is Insarov? Ah, yes, that Serbian or Bulgarian you spoke to me about. The patriot? Perhaps it's from him you get all these philosophical ideas."

"Maybe."

"Is he a remarkable person?"

"He is."

"Intelligent? Gifted?"

"Intelligent? Yes. Gifted? I don't know. I doubt it."

"You doubt it? What is remarkable about him then?"

"You'll see for yourself. I think we ought to go now, Anna Vassilievna is probably waiting for us. What's the time?"

"It's past two. Let's go. How close it is. Our conversation has set my heart on fire. There was a moment when you, too, you. . . . I'm not an artist for nothing; nothing escapes me. . . . Come on, admit that women intrigue you."

Shubin wanted to peer into Bersenev's face, but he turned and walked away from under the lime-tree. Shubin followed him, swinging his small feet gracefully. Bersenev moved clumsily, humping his shoulders as he walked, and sticking out his neck; and yet, in spite of this, he looked more distinguished than Shubin, more like a gentleman, one would say, if the term had not become so hackneyed.

# CHAPTER II

THE YOUNG MEN went down to the river and strolled along the bank. A breath of freshness rose from the water and the soft splash of the small waves caressed the ear.

"I'd like to go in again," Shubin said, "but I'm afraid of being late. Look at the river—it seems to be beckoning to us. The Greeks would have said it's a nymph. But we're not Greeks, O Nymph, we're only thick-skinned Scythians."

"We have our river-fairies," remarked Bersenev.

"River-fairies, indeed! What good are they to me, a sculptor, these figments of a cold and terror-struck imagination, conceived in the stifling atmosphere of a log-hut in the darkness of winter nights? I need light, space. . . . When, oh when, shall I go to Italy? When. . . ."

"You mean when will you go to Little Russia?"

"Shame on you, Andrei Petrovich, to reproach me with my stupid thoughtlessness which I bitterly regret as it is. Of course, I behaved like an idiot. Kind Anna Vassilievna gave me some money to go to Italy, instead of which I went off to eat dumplings in Little Russia and. . . ."

"I'm not interested in what followed," Bersenev broke in.

"But I will say all the same that the money wasn't wasted. I saw such wonderful types there, women particularly. I know, of course, that there's no salvation out-side Italy.''

"You'll go there," murmured Bersenev, turning towards him, "and do nothing, just flap your wings and not fly. I know your sort!"

"Stavasser did fly,* after all. And he wasn't the only one. And if I don't fly it means I'm a penguin, without wings. I'm stifled here, and I want to go to Italy," Shubin continued, "where there's sun and where there's beauty."

A young woman with a broad straw-hat and a pink sun-shade on her shoulder appeared at that moment on the path where the two friends were walking.

"But what do I see? Beauty crossing my path even here! Greetings from a humble artist to the fascinating Zoë!" Shubin suddenly shouted, sweeping his hat off with a theatrical gesture. The young girl to whom this exclama-tion was addressed shook her finger at him, and, when the young men came up close to her, said in a silvery little voice, slightly rolling her r's, "Why don't you come to dinner, gentlemen? It's all ready."

"What do I hear?" Shubin clapped his hands in amazement. "Is it possible that you, the enchanting Zoë, faced this heat in order to find us? Am I right in presuming this? Do I interpret your action correctly? Is it true? Or rather, don't tell me if it isn't—disappointment would kill me on the spot."

"Don't be so silly, Pavel Jakovlevich," the young girl replied, with some irritation. "Why don't you ever speak to me seriously? I'll get really angry with you one day," she added, with a coquettish pout.

* Inventor of a balloon.—*Translator's note.*

14

"You won't get angry, incomparable Zoë Nikitishna, you would not wish to cast me into the dark abyss of abject despair. And I can't speak seriously because I'm not a serious person."

The girl shrugged her shoulders and turned to Bersenev. "He always behaves like that with me; as though I were a child, when I'm already eighteen. Quite grown-up."

"Oh, Heavens!" moaned Shubin and rolled his eyes to the sky, while Bersenev smiled in silence.

The girl stamped her foot. "Pavel Jakovlevich! I'll really lose my temper. . . . Helène was on the point of coming with me," she went on, "but stayed in the garden. The heat was too much for her, but I'm not afraid of the heat. Come along."

And she walked along the path ahead of them, slightly balancing her slim waist at every step and tossing her long soft curls away from her face with a pretty little black-mittened hand.

The two friends followed her (Shubin now silently pressing his hands to his heart, now raising them over his head) and a few minutes later they found themselves in front of one of the numerous summer villas surrounding Kunzovo. A small wooden house with a wing, painted pink, stood in the middle of a garden and peeped out shyly from behind the green foliage. Zoë was the first to open the gate, run into the garden and shout, "I've brought the wanderers!" A young woman with a pale, sensitive face rose from a bench by the side of the path, and a lady in a mauve silk dress appeared on the porch and, lifting an embroidered cambric handkerchief over her head to protect herself from the sun, looked out with a vague and languorous smile on her lips.

# CHAPTER III

ANNA VASSILIEVNA STAKHOVA, *née* Shubin, was orphaned at the age of seven and inherited a fairly considerable property. Some of her relations were very rich, some very poor, poor on her father's side, rich on her mother's, like Senator Volgin, or the Princes Chikurasov. Prince Ardalion Chikurasov, who was appointed her guardian, sent her to one of the best boarding-schools in Moscow and when she had finished there brought her to live in his own home. He kept open house and gave balls in the winter. Anna Vassilievna's future husband, Nikolai Artemievich Stakhov, carried her off by storm at one of these balls when she was wearing an "enchanting pink gown and a head-dress of small roses". She had treasured that head-dress all her life. Nikolai Artemievich Stakhov, son of a retired captain, wounded in 1812 and given a lucrative job in Petersburg, had entered the Military School at the age of sixteen and afterwards went into the Guards. He was handsome, well-built, and considered one of the best dancers at second-best parties, which were those he chiefly frequented, the doors of high society being closed to him. From early youth he had had only two ambitions: one was to become an Imperial A.D.C., the other to make a good marriage. He soon gave up all hope of the first, but clung all the more firmly to the second, and therefore went to Moscow every winter. He spoke passable

French and had the reputation of a philosopher because he was not a rake. Even when he was only an ensign, he used to enjoy starting opinionated arguments—for instance, as to whether a man could manage to go round the world in the course of his lifetime, or whether he could learn what went on at the bottom of the sea, always maintaining the view that it was impossible.

Nikolai Artemievich was twenty-five years old when he "hooked" Anna Vassilievna. He had by then retired to the country in order to manage his property. He soon tired of country life—the land was mortgaged—so he went to live in Moscow, in his wife's house. In his youth he had never played cards or any other games; now he developed a passion for lotto, and when lotto was prohibited, he took a fancy for whist. Home life bored him. He started an affair with a widow of German origin and spent most of his time with her. He did not come to Kunzovo in the summer of '53, but remained in Moscow on the pretext that he had to take the waters—his real reason being that he did not wish to be parted from his widow. They did not waste much of their time talking; though he would occasionally argue about the possibility of forecasting the weather, &c. Somebody once called him a *frondeur*. He liked the sound of the word. Yes, he thought to himself, complacently, turning down the corners of his mouth and rocking on his heels, it's not so easy to please me, or to take me in. His "frondisme" consisted of the following: If someone, for example, mentioned the word "nerves" in his presence, he would say, "What, pray, *are* nerves?" —or if somebody happened to talk about the progress of astronomy he would say, "So you believe in astronomy?" When he wanted to confound his interlocutor, he would

17

say, "It's nothing but words." It has to be admitted that there are people who considered (and still consider) these statements to be irrefutable; it never occurred to Nikolai Artemievich, however, that Augustina Khristianovna, writing to her cousin Feodolinda Petersilius, called him "Mein Pinselchen".

Anna Vassilievna, Nikolai Artemievich's wife, was a thin little woman with fine features and a somewhat emotional and melancholy disposition. At boarding-school she had studied music and read novels, but had later abandoned it all and become absorbed in clothes; they, in their turn, were given up and she took on the education of her daughter, but once again she could not give her mind to it and she handed the child over to a governess. In the end, all she did was to fret and get mildly worked up. Elena Nikolaevna's birth had affected her health and she was not allowed to have any more children. Nikolai Artemievich made discreet insinuations about this to justify his relations with Augustina Khris-tianovna. Her husband's unfaithfulness greatly distressed Anna Vassilievna. She particularly resented the fact that he had once presented his German lady on the sly with a pair of grey roans from Anna Vassilievna's own stables. She never openly reproached him, but secretly com-plained of him to everyone in the house, even to her daughter. She disliked going out and preferred to have guests at home and listen to their stories. Solitude weighed heavily upon her. She had a soft and sensitive heart. She had gone through the mill of life early.

Pavel Jakovlevich Shubin was her cousin three times removed. His father served in Moscow, his brothers all went to military schools. He was the youngest, his

18

mother's favourite, and as he was delicate, he lived at home. He was intended for the University, but it was not without an effort that he managed to scrape through even the secondary school. From his early days he showed a talent for sculpture. One day at his aunt's house the ponderous Senator Volgin saw a statuette which the boy had done at the age of sixteen, and declared that he would encourage this young talent. The sudden death of Shubin's father nearly upset all his future plans. The Senator and patron of the arts presented him with a bust of Homer—that was all—but Anna Vassilievna gave him money and, at nineteen, he managed to get into the Medical School of the University. Not that he had the slightest inclination for medicine, but at the time the quota regulations for students made it impossible to get into any other school. Besides, he wanted to learn a little anatomy. As it happened he did not learn any. He did not pass into his second year and, without waiting for the examination, left the University in order to devote himself entirely to his calling. He was assiduous, but only by fits and starts; he wandered round the outskirts of Moscow; modelled and painted portraits of peasant girls; made friends with various people, young and old, of both high and low estate—Italian modellers and Russian painters—would hear nothing of the Academy and refused to recognize the authority of a single professor. He had a genuine talent and his name became known in Moscow. His mother, who came from a good Parisian family, was a kind-hearted, clever woman. She taught him to speak French, spent days and nights worrying about him and scheming for him, for she was very proud of him. Before her death—she died very young of consumption—she begged Anna Vassilievna to take him under her care. He was then almost twenty-one. Anna Vassilievna carried out her last wish. He occupied a small room in the wing of the villa.

# CHAPTER IV

"DO LET'S GO and eat," the hostess insisted plaintively, and they all moved to the dining room. "Come and sit here, next to me, Zoë," murmured Anna Vassilievna, "And you, Helène, will entertain our guest. As for you, Paul, please don't play any pranks and tease Zoë, I have a migraine to-day."

Shubin again raised his eyes to the ceiling. Zoë responded with a secret smile. This Zoë—or to be more precise, Zoë Nikitishna Mueller—was fair and plump, a nice-looking little Russo-German girl, with a slight squint, a small snub nose, and tiny red lips. She sang Russian songs quite pleasantly; had a neat way of playing various little pieces on the piano, sometimes gay, sometimes sentimental; dressed with taste, if a little too childishly, and with too much primness. Anna Vassilievna had engaged her as companion to her daughter, but kept her almost constantly at her side. Elena made no objection, for she was quite at a loss to know what to say to Zoë whenever they happened to find themselves alone together.

The dinner dragged on for a long time. Bersenev talked to Elena about University life and about his hopes and ambitions. Shubin was all ears, but silent. He ate with exaggerated gluttony, every now and then making comic signs of distress at Zoë who always responded with the same phlegmatic smile. After dinner Elena took Bersenev and Shubin into the garden. Zoë followed them with her eyes and then, with a slight shrug, sat down at the piano. Anna Vassilievna vaguely murmured, "Why don't you go for a stroll, too?" But, without waiting for an answer, added: "Do play something for me, something sad."

"*La Dernière Pensée* de Weber?" suggested Zoë.

"Ah, yes, Weber," Anna Vassilievna whispered softly, as she sank into an armchair, a tear trembling on her lashes.

Elena, in the meantime, had brought the two friends to an arbour under the acacia trees, with a wooden table in the middle surrounded by benches. Shubin had a look round and strolled about, then muttered, "Wait a moment," and rushing to his room came back with some clay and began modelling a statuette of Zoë, shaking his head as he worked, mumbling something under his breath and smiling to himself.

"Up to your old tricks again," said Elena, glancing at his work, and, turning to Bersenev, continued the conversation they'd started at table.

"Old tricks, of course," repeated Shubin. "It's because the subject is so inexhaustible. To-day particularly she gets on my nerves."

"Why's that?" said Elena. "One would think you were speaking of a wicked and disagreeable old woman, not of a pretty young girl. . . ."

"Of course she's pretty," said Shubin, "very pretty indeed. I'm sure that every passer-by glancing at her would say to himself, 'There's someone with whom it would be fun to . . . dance a polka.' I'm equally certain that she knows this and likes it. How do you explain her simpering ways, then, and her coyness? Oh, you know very well what I mean," he added through his

22

teeth, "but you're otherwise engaged at the moment."

And, crushing his model of Zoë, Shubin hurriedly and peevishly began moulding and kneading the clay.

"So you would like to become a professor?" Elena asked Bersenev.

"Yes," he replied, hiding his red hands between his knees, "that's my fond hope. I'm well aware, of course, how ill-equipped I am to aspire to such heights. I mean, I haven't been adequately prepared, though I hope to be allowed to go abroad soon and I'll stay there three or four years if necessary and then. . . ."

He stopped and looked down, then with a brusque gesture raised his eyes to her with an awkward smile and brushed back his hair. When Bersenev spoke to a woman, his speech became even more halting, his lisp more pronounced.

"You want to become a professor of history?" asked Elena.

"Yes, that or philosophy," he added, lowering his voice, "if possible."

"He's a perfect devil at philosophy already," remarked Shubin, making deep marks in the clay with his nail, "there's no point in his going abroad for that."

"And then you'd be perfectly happy?" asked Elena, resting her cheek on her hand and looking him straight in the face.

"Perfectly happy, Elena Nikolaevna, perfectly happy. Could one have a better profession? Just think, to follow in the footsteps of Timofei Nikolaevich*. . . . The mere thought of such a career fills me with joy and dismay, yes

---

* T. N. Granovski (1813-55), an eminent historian of Moscow University.—*Translator's note.*

. . . dismay . . . because . . . because I'm conscious of my shortcomings. My father gave it his blessing. I shall never forget his last words.''

''Your father died this winter?''

''Yes, Elena Nikolaevna, in February.''

''I hear he left a remarkable work in manuscript, isn't that so?'' continued Elena.

''Yes, he did, he was a wonderful man. You would have loved him, Elena Nikolaevna.''

''I'm sure I would. What was the work about?''

''It's difficult to tell you in a few words, Elena Nikolaevna. My father was a very learned man, a disciple of Schelling. He liked using obscure terms. . . .''

''Andrei Petrovich,'' Elena interrupted him, ''forgive my ignorance, but what exactly is a disciple of Schelling?''

''Schelling was a German philosopher,'' Bersenev answered with a faint smile. ''His teaching was. . . .''

''Andrei Petrovich!'' Shubin exclaimed, ''for mercy's sake. Do you really propose giving Elena Nikolaevna a lecture on Schelling? Have a heart.''

''Not a lecture at all,'' explained Bersenev, blushing furiously, ''I merely wanted. . . .''

''And why not a lecture?'' Elena retorted. ''It would do us no harm, Pavel Jakovlevich.''

Shubin stared at her and all of a sudden burst out laughing.

''What are you laughing at?'' she asked coldly, almost sharply.

Shubin was silent. ''Now don't be angry with me,'' he went on after a while, ''I plead guilty. But do you really want to talk philosophy now, on such a night, under these trees? Wouldn't you rather talk about nightingales and roses, and young eyes that smile?''

24

"Yes, and why not add French novels and women's fashions," continued Elena.

"Why not women's fashions if they are attractive," retorted Shubin.

"By all means, but supposing we don't want to talk about fashions? You speak of your independence as an artist. Why, then, won't you let other people do as they please? And if this is the way you think, may I ask why you find fault with Zoë? She's just the person to discuss dresses and roses with."

Shubin suddenly flared up and leapt to his feet. "So that's what it is?" he began unsteadily. "I can take a hint, Elena Nikolaevna. You want me to go to her. I am *de trop* here. . . ."

"I mean nothing of the sort."

"You wish to imply," Shubin continued hotly, "that I'm not worthy of any other companionship, that she and I make a good pair, that I'm just as vain, frivolous and petty as that cloying little German. Isn't that so?"

Elena frowned. "You didn't always have such a poor opinion of her, Pavel Jakovlevich," she remarked.

"Ah, now we come to reproaches!" Shubin exclaimed. "Well, yes, I'll admit that there was a moment, no more than a moment, when her vulgar, chubby little cheeks . . . . But what if I returned the reproach and reminded you. . . . Goodbye!" he concluded suddenly, "or I might say more than I mean." And, striking the piece of clay he had moulded into the shape of a head, he rushed out of the arbour and up to his room.

"What a baby!" Elena murmured, following him with a glance.

"An artist," Bersenev observed with a quiet smile.

"They're all like that. We have to forgive them their whims. They have a right to them."

"Yes," Elena replied, "but Pavel has not yet qualified for it. What has he done up to now? Give me your arm and let's walk down this path. He interrupted us. We were talking about your father's work."

Bersenev gave Elena his arm and they strolled into the garden; but the conversation, interrupted before it had got going, was not resumed. Bersenev once again spoke of his professorial calling, of his future work. He moved slowly at Elena's side with an awkward gait, awkwardly supporting her arm, occasionally bumping against her shoulder and never once glancing at her. But he spoke easily, if not quite freely. He talked with simple conviction and his eyes, slowly travelling along the trunks of the trees, over the sand of the path and the grass, shone with that exalted look which springs from noble thoughts, while his calm voice expressed the joy of one who finds himself able to open his heart to someone very dear to him. Elena listened to him attentively, her head half turned towards him, and never moved her eyes away from his face, which had suddenly become pale, nor from his gentle and friendly eyes which avoided hers. Her soul seemed to expand, and something warm, true and good seemed to flow into her heart or to well up inside it.

# CHAPTER  V

SHUBIN DID NOT leave his room till late that night. It was already quite dark, the semicircle of the moon stood high in the sky, the Milky Way was a white shadow, and the stars glimmered here and there, when Bersenev, having taken leave of Anna Vassilievna, Elena and Zoë, came to his friend's door. He found it bolted and gave a knock.

"Who's there?" Shubin called.

"It's me," said Bersenev.

"What do you want?"

"Let me in, Pavel. Stop being capricious. Aren't you ashamed of yourself?"

"I'm not being capricious, I'm asleep and dreaming of Zoë."

"Stop this nonsense. You're behaving like a child. Let me in. I must talk to you."

"Haven't you talked enough with Elena?"

"Now, really, don't be a fool. Let me in."

Shubin replied with a pretence at snoring.

Bersenev shrugged his shoulders and went home.

The night was warm and strangely silent, as though everything around were on the watch, listening. Bersenev, wrapped in the motionless mist, could not help stopping now and then, to watch and listen, too. A slight swish, like the rustle of a woman's dress which could be heard from time to time among the nearby tree-tops, gave him a deliciously eerie feeling akin to fear. His cheeks tingled, and his eyes filled with cold tears; he longed to tread noiselessly, to keep out of sight, to move stealthily. When a sudden breeze blew from one side, he shivered slightly and stood still; a drowsy beetle tumbled off a branch and fell with a thud on to the path. Bersenev exclaimed softly and stopped again. Then he began thinking of Elena and all these passing sensations vanished immediately, leaving behind only the stimulating feeling of the night's freshness and of walking at night. The image of the young girl possessed his thoughts completely. Bersenev walked on, with his head bent, recalling her words and her questions. He seemed to hear behind him the sound of hurried steps. He pricked up his ears. Somebody was running, trying to catch up with him—he could hear the uneven breathing. Suddenly, in front of him, out of the black circle of shadow cast by a large tree, Shubin emerged, looking very pale in the moonlight, and without a hat on his dishevelled hair.

"I'm glad you took this path," he managed to blurt out; "I shouldn't have slept a wink the whole night if I hadn't caught up with you. Give me your hand. You're going home, aren't you?"

"Yes, I am."

"I'll come with you."

"But how can you, without a hat?"

"It doesn't matter. I haven't got a cravat either. It's warm now."

The two friends walked on for a while.

"I behaved very stupidly today, didn't I?" Shubin asked suddenly.

"To tell you the truth, you did. I couldn't make you

out. I'd never seen you like that. And what was it that made you so angry? Some trifle, I suppose?"

"Hm . . ." muttered Shubin, "you may think so, but it isn't a trifling matter for me. You see," he added, "I must tell you that I . . . that. . . . You may think what you like of me, but I . . . yes . . . . I'm in love with Elena."

"You're in love with Elena?" repeated Bersenev, and stopped short.

"Yes," Shubin went on with affected indifference. "Are you surprised? I can go further and tell you that until tonight, I had reason to hope she might, in time, return my love . . . but tonight I realized that I haven't the slightest chance. She has fallen in love with someone else. . . ."

"With someone else? But who?"

"Who? With you!" Subin exclaimed and slapped Bersenev on the shoulder.

"With me?"

"With you," repeated Shubin.

Bersenev took a step backwards and stood quite still. Shubin looked at him closely.

"Are you surprised? You're a modest young man. Anyway, she loves you, you can be sure of that."

"What nonsense you talk!" Bersenev exclaimed at last with annoyance.

"It's far from being nonsense. Why are we standing, by the way? Come on, it's much easier to talk as we go along. I've known her for a long time and know her well. I can't be mistaken. You're somebody after her own heart. There was a time when I attracted her, but to begin with I'm too flippant a young man for her taste, whereas you're a

29

serious person, a physically and mentally tidy individual, you're. . . . Wait a moment, I haven't finished. You're a determined but well-balanced enthusiast, a true representative of those high-priests of science on whom—no, I should say whereon the average Russian gentry so legitimately prides itself. In the second place. . . . Elena caught me the other day kissing . . . Zoë's arms!"

"Zoë's arms?"

"Yes, what can one do if she has such splendid shoulders?"

"Shoulders?"

"Yes, yes, what does it matter—arms, shoulders? Elena caught me at these liberal exercises after dinner, and before dinner I'd been abusing Zoë in her presence. Unfortunately, Elena doesn't understand that such contradictions are perfectly natural. Then you turned up. You believe in—what is it, actually, that you believe in?—you blush, you're shy, you talk about Schelling, about Schiller (she's always on the look-out for remarkable people)—so it's obvious that you win, while I, miserable wretch that I am, try to joke, while . . ."

Shubin suddenly burst into tears, walked away, sat down on the ground and clutched at his hair.

Bersenev went up to him. "Pavel," he began, "what is this childish behaviour? Pull yourself together. What's the matter with you to-day? God alone knows what nonsense has got into your head, and now you're crying. I really believe you're pretending."

Shubin raised his head. Tears glistened on his cheeks in the moonlight, but his face was smiling.

"Andrei Petrovich," he said, "you may think what you like about me. I'm ready to admit that I'm hysterical

30

at this moment, but I swear I'm in love with Elena and Elena is in love with you. Anyway, I've promised to see you back home and I'll keep my promise."

He got up. "What a night! A silvery, dark, young night. How beautiful it is for those who are loved. How delightful it is for them to stay awake. Will you sleep, Andrei Petrovich?"

Bersenev did not reply and quickened his pace.

"What's all the hurry about?" continued Shubin; "believe me, you won't have another night like this in your life—and at home you'll only find Schelling. It's true that he came in useful for you to-day. All the same, don't hurry, sing as loudly as you can, if you can sing at all, and if you can't, take off your hat, throw your head back, and smile up at the stars. They're all staring at you and at you only. They do nothing but stare at people who are in love—that's why they are so charming—for you *are* in love, aren't you, Andrei Petrovich? No answer? Why don't you answer?" Shubin went on. "Oh, but if you're happy, say nothing, say nothing. I babble on because I'm the unloved one, the wretched one, the clown, the artist, the mountebank; but what unspeakable delight would I not absorb from these nocturnal influences, under these stars, if I only knew that someone loved me. Bersenev, are you happy?"

Bersenev remained silent and walked on quickly along the smooth road. In front of him, among the trees, flickered the lights of the village where he lived. It consisted of a dozen small summer villas. There was a village shop at the beginning of it, on the right hand side of the road, under two spreading birch-trees. The windows in it were already closed, but a broad patch of light from the

B*                            31

half-open door lay fanwise on the trodden grass and stretched as far as the trees, sharply illuminating the whitish underside of their thick foliage. A young girl, apparently a house-maid, was standing in the shop with her back to the door, bargaining with the shop-keeper; her round cheeks and slender neck were hardly visible under the red scarf she had thrown over her head and was holding with her bare arm under her chin. The two young men came into the patch of light. Shubin peered into the shop, stopped, and called out, "Annushka!"

The girl turned round abruptly, revealing a pretty face. It was a full, fresh face, with gay, brown eyes and black eyebrows.

"Annushka!" Shubin repeated.

The girl looked at him more intently, became frightened, seemed overcome with shyness, and, without completing her purchase, quickly stepped down from the porch, slipped past hurriedly and walked over to the left-hand side of the road, glancing nervously over her shoulder. The puffy shop-keeper, indifferent to the world like all suburban shop-keepers, grunted and looked after her with a yawn, while Shubin turned to Bersenev and said: "There's . . . you see, there's . . . a family here I happen to know . . . so . . . so they . . . don't imagine now. . . ." And, without completing his speech, he ran after the disappearing girl.

"Wipe away your tears, at least," Bersenev shouted after him, and could not help laughing. But when he got home, he was not laughing any more. There was no trace of merriment on his face. Although he had not believed for a moment what Shubin had told him, his words had sunk deep into his heart. "Pavel was making fun of me,"

32

he thought. "One day, though, she will fall in love. Who will she fall in love with?"

Bersenev had a piano in his room, a small, second-hand piano, with a soft and pleasant but not very clear tone. He sat down at it and tried some chords. Like all Russian noblemen, he had had music lessons in his childhood; like almost all Russian noblemen he played very badly, but was passionately fond of music. As a matter of fact, what he liked about it was neither the technique nor the medium (symphonies and sonatas, even operas made him feel gloomy) but its elemental quality. He loved the vague, sweet, impersonal, comprehensive emotions which the combination and interplay of sounds stirred up inside him. For more than an hour he sat at the piano, repeating the same chords over and over again, clumsily trying to find new ones, pausing, then fading out on a diminished seventh. His heart ached and his eyes frequently filled with tears. He was not ashamed of them as they fell in the darkness. "Pavel is right," he thought, "I feel that this evening will never be repeated." At last he got up, lit a candle, put on a dressing-gown, fetched from the shelf the second volume of Raumer's *History of the Hohenstaufens*, and after sighing several times, began to read diligently.

# CHAPTER VI

MEANWHILE, ELENA RETURNED to her room, sat down by the open window and propped her face on her hands. It had become a habit with her to spend about a quarter of an hour at her window every evening. She had a talk with herself in the time, during which she summed up the day that had gone by. She had just reached the age of twenty. She was tall; she had a pale, sallow complexion, large, grey eyes under arched eyebrows, with tiny freckles all round them, a perfectly straight forehead and nose, firm lips and a rather sharp chin. She wore her dark brown hair in a plait low on the nape of her slender neck. Everything about her—the expression of her face, tense and slightly anxious; the direct but changing glance; the seemingly strained smile; the soft but hesitating voice— suggested something electric and febrile, something impulsive and hasty—in a word, something which was not to everybody's taste, which even repelled many people. Her hands were slender, rose-pink, with long tapering fingers. Her feet were slender, too; she walked briskly, almost impetuously, with a slight forward tilt. She had developed in an unusual way: at first she had worshipped her father, had then become passionately attached to her mother, and had later grown indifferent to both of them, her father in particular. She now behaved towards her mother as one does towards an ailing grandparent. Her

34

father, who had been proud of her while she was considered an exceptional child, began, now that she was grown-up, to be afraid of her and said of her, "Heaven only knows how she comes to be such an advanced *républicaine*!" She had no patience with any form of weakness, nor could she suffer fools gladly; she would never, never forgive a lie; she was relentless in her demands; even her prayers were often mingled with reproaches. If anyone fell in her estimation—and she was quick, sometimes too quick, in her judgement—they ceased to exist for her. Everything she felt made a deep impression on her. Life was not an easy business for her.

The governess whom Anna Vassilievna had entrusted with the finishing touches to her daughter's education—an education which, we may note in parenthesis, her mother, who suffered easily from *ennui*, had never had the energy to begin—was a Russian, the daughter of an impecunious and corrupt official. She had been educated at a girls' high school and was a kind, sentimental and deceitful creature. She was constantly falling in love and ended by marrying, in the year 1850, when Elena was seventeen, an officer of sorts, who promptly abandoned her. She loved literature and every now and then turned out small poems of her own. She awakened in Elena a taste for reading, but reading by itself was not enough. From childhood on, Elena yearned for a life of strenuous activity and active benevolence. The poor, the sick, the hungry, were constantly in her thoughts, tormenting and torturing her, pursuing her in her dreams. She questioned all her friends about them and, almost trembling with concern, distributed alms with great solicitude and unconscious solemnity. All ill-treated animals, starved watch-dogs, kittens doomed to death, sparrows which had fallen out of their nests, even snakes and insects, found shelter and protection with Elena. She fed them herself and never found them repellent. Her mother did not interfere with her, but her father was outraged by what he called his daughter's vulgar sentimentality, and maintained that one could not move in the house for cats and dogs. "Lenochka,"* he would call out to her, "hurry up, a spider is hurting a fly, come and set the miserable creature free." And Lenochka, very much perturbed, ran along and released the fly by disengaging its tiny legs. "Well, as you're so kind, why not let it have a bite at you now?" her father remarked ironically, but she didn't listen to him. When she was nine, she made friends with a little beggar-girl, Katia, and used to meet her secretly in the garden, bring her sweets, give her a little money, a few handkerchiefs—Katia would not take toys. She sat down next to her on the dry ground, hiding behind a thick growth of nettles and, with a feeling of blissful humility, ate her stale bread and listened to her stories. Katia had an aunt, a wicked old woman, who often used to beat her. Katia hated her and never stopped talking about how she would run away from her and live in "God's full freedom". Elena listened to these strange, new words with secret admiration and fear; as she stared fixedly at Katia, everything about her—her quick, black, almost feline eyes, her sunburnt arms, her husky voice, even her tattered frock—seemed wonderful to Elena, almost holy. She would go home and sit thinking for a long time about beggars, about God's freedom; dream about cutting a stick for herself from a walnut tree, about taking a beggar's sack and running away with Katia, wandering about the

* Diminutive for Elena.—*Translator's note.*

roads with a wreath of cornflowers in her hair—she had once seen Katia weaving one. If one of the family entered the room at such a moment, she looked sulky and morose. One day she ran out to meet Katia in the rain and dirtied her frock. Her father, seeing her like that, called her a ill-bred slut. She flushed scarlet—a mixture of fear and happiness welled up inside her. Katia often hummed a coarse little soldiers' song. Elena picked it up from her. Anna Vassilievna heard it and was horrified. "Where did you pick up such dreadful stuff?" she asked her daughter. Elena merely looked at her mother and never uttered a word; she felt she would rather let herself be torn to pieces than reveal her secret; and again fear and happiness stole into her heart.

Her friendship with Katia did not last long, however. The poor little girl caught a pernicious fever and died after a few days. Elena was very upset, and for a long time after learning about Katia's death she could not sleep at night. The little beggar-girl's last words constantly rang in her ears and it seemed to her that someone was calling her.

The years went by. Rapidly, noiselessly, like water under the snow, Elena's youth rushed past, in outward idleness, in inner struggle and anxiety. She had no friends, she had formed no ties with any of the girls that visited the Stakhovs' house. Her parents' authority never counted much with Elena and after the age of sixteen she became almost completely independent. She lived her own life, but it was a lonely life. Her soul flared up and the flame died down, but always in solitude. She fluttered like a bird in a cage, only there was no cage—nobody restrained her, nobody coerced her—yet she wistfully longed to tear

herself away. Sometimes she could not understand herself, sometimes was even frightened of herself. Everything
around her seemed either meaningless or inexplicable.
"How can one live without love—and there is no one to
love!" she thought and was terrified by such thoughts and
impressions. When she was eighteen she almost died of a
malignant fever. Her constitution, shaken to the core,
though naturally strong and healthy, could not throw it
off for a long time. Even when the last symptoms of the
illness had finally disappeared, her father still spoke, not
without irritation, about her "nerves". Sometimes it
seemed to her that she longed for something that no one
else desired, that no one else dreamt of in the whole of
Russia. Then she would calm down, even laugh at herself
and spend one carefree day after another, until suddenly
some indefinable pressure which she could not control
rose in her and craved to be released. Then the storm
would pass and she would fold her tired but untried wings.
She paid a heavy price for these emotional outbursts, for,
however much she tried not to give away what was going
on inside her, her outward calm was itself a symptom of
inner anguish and distress. Her parents therefore, unable
to understand her "queerness", were often justified in
shrugging their shoulders in bewilderment.

On the day our story began, Elena stayed longer than
usual at the window. She thought a lot about Bersenev,
about her talk with him. She liked him, she believed in
the warmth of his feelings, in the sincerity of his aims. He
had never spoken to her before as he had that evening.
She remembered the expression of his timid eyes, his
smile, and then she, too, smiled and became thoughtful,
but her thoughts were not with Bersenev. She looked out

"into the night" through the open window. For a long time she gazed at the dark, overhanging sky. Then she rose, shook back the hair from her face, and without knowing why, stretched out her cool, bare arms to the sky, then let them drop, knelt down by the side of her bed, pressed her face to the pillow and, in spite of her effort to fight against the emotion that possessed her, burst into an inexplicable, confused and passionate flood of tears.

# CHAPTER VII

THE NEXT DAY, about noon, Bersenev left for Moscow in a hired carriage which was making the return journey. He had to collect some money from the post-office and buy some books; he also wanted to see Insarov and talk to him. During his last talk with Shubin it had occurred to him to invite Insarov to stay in his country lodgings. It took him some time, however, to get in touch with his friend. He had moved from his previous quarters to others which were not easy to find; they were in the backyard of a hideous stone house built in the Petersburg style, between the Arbat and the Povarskaia. In vain did Bersenev wander from one dirty porch to another, in vain did he call out to the door-keeper, or to "whoever's there". Door-keepers even in Petersburg, and all the more so in Moscow, try to avoid being spotted by visitors, so nobody answered Bersenev; only an inquisitive tailor in a waistcoat, with a piece of grey thread on his shoulder, and a black eye, silently poked his blank, unshaven face out of a top case-ment window; and a black, hornless goat, perched on a dung heap, turned towards Bersenev, emitted a plaintive bleat, and began chewing the cud faster than ever. Finally, a woman in an old dressing-gown and down-trodden shoes took pity on him and pointed out where Insarov lived. Bersenev found him at home. He rented a room in the flat of the same tailor who had stared out of the window and

taken so little interest in the wanderer and his difficulties—
a large, almost empty room with dark green walls, three
square windows, a tiny bed in one corner, a small leather
couch in the other, and a huge cage hanging high up under
the ceiling. A nightingale had once lived in it. Insarov got
up to greet Bersenev as soon as he crossed the threshold,
but he did not exclaim, "Ah, it's you!" or "What's
brought you here, by God?"—he did not even say "How
do you do?", but merely pressed his hand and led him to
the only chair in the room.

"Sit down" he said, and perched himself on the edge
of the table. "As you see, everything is still upside down
here," he added, pointing to the heap of papers and books
on the floor; "I haven't properly settled down yet.
Haven't had time."

Insarov spoke Russian quite correctly, pronouncing
every word clearly and distinctly, but his guttural voice,
though pleasant, sounded somehow un-Russian. His
foreign origin (he was Bulgarian) showed even more in
his appearance: he was a young man of about twenty-five
years of age, gaunt and angular, with a hollow chest and
knobbly hands; he had striking features, an aquiline nose,
very straight black hair, a low forehead, thick eyebrows,
small deep-set eyes with a fixed expression in them. When
he smiled he revealed for a moment a set of dazzling white
teeth between lips which were thin and firm and too
sharply defined. The jacket he wore was old but neat and
was buttoned up to the neck.

"Why did you leave your last lodgings?" Bersenev
asked him.

"These are cheaper and nearer to the University."

"But we're right in the middle of the vacation at the

41

moment. And what's the point of living in town in the summer? Why didn't you take rooms in the country, as you'd decided to move?"

Insarov did not reply to this remark and offered Bersenev a pipe, adding that he was sorry not to have any cigars or cigarettes. Bersenev lit the pipe.

"As for me," he went on, "I've taken a small house near Kunzovo. Very cheap, very comfortable. I've even got a spare-room upstairs."

Insarov still remained silent. Bersenev drew at his pipe.

"It even occurred to me," he continued, letting out a thin cloud of smoke, "that if, for instance, someone would . . . you, for example, I thought . . . would like, would care to take up quarters in that top room of mine . . . how nice it would be! What do you think of it, Dmitri Nikanorich?"

Insarov glanced up at him with his small eyes.

"You're suggesting that I should come and live in your house?"

"Yes, on the top floor where there's a spare-room."

"I'm very grateful to you, Andrei Petrovich, but I'm afraid my means wouldn't run to it."

"How do you mean, not run to it?"

"Not run to my living in a country house. I couldn't afford two places."

"But . . ." began Bersenev, and stopped short. "You would have no additional expenses connected with it," he continued, "you would keep on this room, let us say, but everything is very cheap over there and we could even arrange, for instance, to have our meals together."

Insarov was silent again and Bersenev felt embarrassed.

"In any case, come and visit me sometime," he began

42

after a pause. "There's a family living there a stone's throw away from me which I'd so much like to introduce you to. If only you knew, Insarov, what a wonderful young daughter they have. A close friend of mine also lives with them, a man of great talent. I feel certain that you would get on well with him. (A Russian loves lavishing things on one—if there is nothing else, he will lavish his friends.) No, seriously, do come. Better still, come and stay with me. We could work together and read. You know I'm studying history and philosophy. I know you're interested in all these things. I've a large collection of books."

Insarov got up and walked about the room.

"May I ask," he inquired at last, "what you pay for your house?"

"One hundred silver roubles."

"And how many rooms have you got in it?"

"Five."

"So that would make, I reckon, twenty roubles for the room?"

"It would. . . . But look here, I don't use it at all. It just stands empty."

"Perhaps, but listen to me," added Insarov, with a firm and at the same time artless movement of the head, "I can accept your offer if you agree to take the money. I can afford twenty roubles, particularly if you say that I can economise on things over there."

"But of course, only this is very embarrassing."

"I'm sorry, Andrei Petrovich, I can't agree to anything else."

"Well, have it your own way, but how stubborn you are." Insarov again did not reply.

The young men fixed the day when Insarov was to make the move. The landlord was summoned, but he first sent his daughter, a little girl of seven with a huge check shawl over her head, to talk to them. She listened attentively, almost in terror, to all that Insarov said to her and went away without a word. She was followed by her mother, who was in the last stages of pregnancy, and who also had a shawl, but this time a tiny one, round her head. Insarov explained to her that he was moving to a house near Kunzovo, but keeping on his room and leaving all his belongings in her care. The tailor's wife also seemed to listen in terror and went away in her turn. At last the landlord himself came. He seemed to understand everything straight away and at the end merely repeated, wistfully, "Near Kunzovo?" But as soon as he had left them, he suddenly opened the door again and shouted, "What about the room, keeping it, are you?" Insarov reassured him. "I've got to know, see," the tailor repeated sullenly, and disappeared from sight.

Bersenev set off home, very pleased with the success of his proposal. Insarov accompanied him to the door, with a politeness not often practised in Russia, and, when he was alone again, removed his jacket carefully and began to sort his papers.

# CHAPTER VIII

ON THE EVENING of the same day Anna Vassilievna was sitting in her drawing-room, working herself up for a good cry. With her in the room were her husband and a certain Uvar Ivanovich Stakhov, a distant cousin of Nikolai Artemievich, a retired cornet of sixty, a man immobilized by corpulence, with small sleepy yellow eyes and fat colourless lips in a bloated yellow face. From the time of his retirement he had always lived in Moscow on the income of a little capital left him by his wife who was of the merchant class. He did nothing and it is doubtful whether he ever indulged in thinking; anyway, if he did think, he kept his thoughts to himself. Only once in his life did he get excited and show some activity. It was after having read in the newspapers about a new instrument at the Great Exhibition in London, the "Contrabombardon". He wanted to buy this instrument and even made inquiries as to where the money should be transferred and through what agency. Uvar Ivanovich wore a loose tobacco-coloured coat and a white cravat round his neck. He was a frequent and copious feeder and in moments of perplexity, that is to say whenever he had to express an opinion, he would make a convulsive movement in the air with the fingers of his right hand, first from the thumb to the little finger, then from the little finger to the thumb, adding with an effort, "One should . . . somehow . . . that is . . . ."

Uvar Ivanovich sat in an armchair by the window, breathing stertorously. Nikolai Artemievich strode up and down the room, his hands pushed into his pockets, his face showing signs of displeasure. He stopped at last and shook his head.

"Yes," he said, "in our day young people were brought up differently. Young people wouldn't have let themselves show disrespect to their elders." (He pronounced "disrespect" in his nose, in a French way.)* "Now I just sit back and look on with amazement. Perhaps I'm wrong and they're right. Maybe. But I'm entitled to my point of view, am I not? I was not born a boor, after all. What do you think about it, Uvar Ivanovich?"

Uvar Ivanovich merely looked at him and twiddled his fingers.

"For instance, take Elena Nikolaevna," continued Nikolai Artemievich, "I can't make her out, really I can't. I'm not sufficiently elevated for her. Her heart is so capacious that it embraces the whole of Nature down to the last beetle or frog—in a word, everything but her own father. Very well, I'm aware of this and I let it pass. Because all these nerves and education and living in the clouds—they're not in my line. But that Mr. Shubin . . . even admitting that he's a remarkable, a wonderful artist —I won't argue about that— . . . that Mr. Shubin should show disrespect to an older man to whom, whatever one may say, he owes a lot, this, dans mon gros bon sens, I cannot allow. I'm not exacting by nature, but there's a limit to everything."

* In Russian—mankirovat—a Gallicism: manquer de respect — *Translator's note.*

Anna Vassilievna nervously rang the bell. A pageboy came in.

"Why doesn't Pavel Jakovlevich come?" she said, "Why can't I get him to come?"

Nikolai Artemievich shrugged his shoulders. "Why, pray, do you want him to come? I'm not asking you to see him, I don't even want to see him."

"How can you ask why, Nikolai Artemicvich? He has upset you, he may even have interfered with your cure. I want him to explain, I want to know what he has done to annoy you."

"I repeat that I'm not asking you to do that. And why on earth devant les domestiques. . . ."

Anna Vassilievna flushed slightly. "You're wrong, Nikolai Artemievich, I never . . . devant . . . les . . . domestiques. Fediusha, go and bring Pavel Jakovlevich here at once."

The pageboy left the room.

"It's all quite unnecessary," Nikolai Artemievich muttered through his teeth, and began to walk up and down the room again. "I wasn't going to bring all this up."

"But, my dear, Pavel must apologize to you."

"Pray, what do I need his apologies for? And what are apologies? Nothing but phrases."

"But what do you mean? Surely you must want to give him a piece of your mind."

"*You* can do that. He'll be more likely to listen to you. I've got nothing against him."

"Now, Nikolai Artemievich, you've been in a bad mood ever since you arrived to-day. In my opinion you've even grown thinner. I'm afraid that your cure doesn't agree with you."

"My cure is essential to me," remarked Nikolai Artemievich; "my liver is in a poor condition."

At that moment Shubin came in. He seemed tired, there was a faint, mocking smile on his lips.

"You were asking for me, Anna Vassilievna?" he murmured.

"Yes, I did ask for you. Pavel, this is dreadful. I'm very displeased with you. I hear that you've been disrespectful to Nikolai Artemievich."

"Has Nikolai Artemievich complained about me?" asked Shubin, and with the same mocking smile glanced at Stakhov. The latter turned away and lowered his eyes.

"Yes, he did complain. I don't know what you have done to upset him, but you must apologize at once because his health is not at all what it should be, and also because we must all show respect to our benefactors when we're young."

"What logic!" Shubin thought to himself and turned to Stakhov. "I'm ready to apologize to you, Nikolai Artemievich," he said with a polite bow, "if I have really offended you in some way."

"I wasn't . . . really . . ." Nikolai Artemievich replied, continuing to avoid Shubin's eyes, "but anyway, I forgive you readily, because you know I'm not an exacting person."

"Oh, there's never been any doubt about that," murmured Shubin, "but may I be allowed to ask whether Anna Vassilievna is aware of the manner in which I have sinned?"

"No, I know nothing," said Anna Vassilievna, stretching out her neck.

"Oh, heavens above!" Nikolai Artemievich exclaimed

48

hastily, "how many times have I begged, implored, how often have I repeated that I dislike these scenes and explanations! One comes home once in a while to have a rest, one is told how fine it is to be a family man, in your *intérieur*, in the bosom of your family—and all one gets is scenes and unpleasantness. Not a moment's peace. No wonder a man goes to his club..or..or..elsewhere. A man is human, after all, with a body that makes certain demands on him, while. . . ." And without finishing his speech, Nikolai Artemievich strode out of the room and banged the door. Anna Vassilievna followed him with a glance.

"To the club!" she murmured bitterly. "It isn't the club you're going to, you philanderer. It isn't there that you will find someone to give horses to, from *my* stables, and grey ones at that! My favourite colour! Yes, you fickle creature," she added, raising her voice, "it's not the club you're going to. And you, too, Pavel," she continued, rising from her chair, "aren't you ashamed of yourself? After all, you're not a child. Now I've got a headache again. Where's Zoë, do you know?"

"In her room upstairs, I believe. The sly little vixen always hides in her earth in this weather."

"Now, now, that's enough!" Anna Vassilievna looked round the room: "Have you seen my little flask with the grated horseradish? Paul, I beg of you, don't make me angry in future!"

"Why should I make you angry, my dear aunt! Let me kiss your hand. And I saw your horseradish on the table in the study."

"Daria always forgets it somewhere," murmured Anna Vassilievna, and went out with her silk dress rustling.

Shubin was about to follow her, but stopped, hearing behind him the slow voice of Uvar Ivanovich.

"You nincompoop . . . you ought to have got it proper . . ." the retired cornet hummed and hawed.

Shubin went up to him. "What should I have got it proper for, my good Uvar Ivanovich?"

"What for? You're young, so you ought to show respect. Yes."

"For whom?"

"Who? You know very well who. No point in grinning like that."

Shubin folded his arms across his chest. "Ah, you perfect representative of the herd instinct, you elemental force of the black earth, you foundation stone of society!"

Uvar Ivanovich began playing with his fingers. "That's enough, my boy, don't lead me into temptation."

"Here's a nobleman of mature years," continued Shubin, "and behold how much childish, happy faith he still has! Respect, indeed! Do you know, you elemental creature, why Nikolai Artemievich has seen fit to be angry with me to-day? I spent the whole morning with him and his German lady; we sang 'Oh, never leave me' as a trio. If only you'd heard us! I believe you're susceptible to that sort of thing. Well, my dear sir, we went on singing and singing—and I got bored, I could see it was all going wrong—far too much sentiment about it. So I started teasing them. It was a great success. First she got angry with me, then with him, then he got angry with her and said that the only place where he was ever happy was at home, which was paradise itself, and she then told him that he had no morals. So I said, "Ach!" to her in German, upon which he left and I stayed behind. He came back here, that is, to his paradise, and his paradise doesn't seem to suit him and that's why he's grumbling. So now, who would you say is to blame?"

"You, of course," replied Uvar Ivanovich.

Shubin stared at him. "May I inquire, oh worthy knight," he began in an obsequious manner, "whether you condescended to utter those enigmatic words as a result of an exercise of your mental faculties, or under the impulse of a sudden desire to produce a vibration in the air, called a sound?"

"I repeat, don't tempt me!" groaned Uvar Ivanovich.

Shubin laughed and ran out of the room. A quarter of an hour later, Uvar Ivanovich exclaimed, "Heh! What about a glass of vodka. . . ."

The pageboy brought some vodka and a snack on a tray. Uvar Ivanovich slowly took the glass from the tray and gazed at it for a long time with a great effort of concentration as though wondering what it was that he was holding in his hand. Then he glanced at the pageboy and asked "Isn't your name Vasska?" He then pulled a long face, drank the vodka and took a bite of something and shoved his hand into his pocket in search of a handkerchief. But the pageboy had long ago taken the tray and the decanter back to where they belonged and eaten the remaining bit of herring, in fact, he was already asleep, leaning against the gentleman's overcoat, while Uvar Ivanovich still held the handkerchief spread out on his fingers and gaped with the same concentrated attention now at the window, now at the walls, or at the floor.

## CHAPTER IX

SHUBIN RETURNED TO his wing of the house and was
on the point of picking up a book. Nikolai Artemievich's
valet walked cautiously into the room and handed him a
small triangle of paper with a large seal on it. "I hope,"
the note said, "that, as a man of honour, you will not
divulge by the smallest hint the matter of the I.O.U.
which was the subject of this morning's conversation.
You know my way of looking at things and my standards,
the insignificance of the sum and other circumstances.
Also there are family secrets which have to be respected
and family peace is something so sacred that only
'des êtres sans coeur', of which I have no reason to
consider you one, can possibly deny it. (Return this
note.) N.S."

Shubin scribbled underneath it in pencil, "Have no
fear, I'm not yet in the habit of pinching handkerchiefs out
of pockets," gave the note back to the valet and picked up
his book again. But it soon slipped out of his hands. He
glanced at the rose-pale sky, at the two strong young fir-
trees standing isolated from the other ones, thought to
himself, "Fir-trees have a bluish hue by day and how
beautifully green they are by night!", and went to the
garden in the secret hope of finding Elena there. He was
not disappointed. Ahead of him, on the path through the
shrubbery, he caught a glimpse of her frock. He caught up

with her and, coming alongside, murmured, "Don't look in my direction, I'm not worth it."

She gave him a swift glance, a swift smile and walked on into the heart of the garden. Shubin followed her.

"I beg you not to look at me, and then I go on speaking to you," he began: "an obvious inconsistency! But that's of no importance. It's not the first time it has happened to me. I've just remembered that I haven't yet apologized to you properly after my stupid behaviour yesterday. Are you angry with me, Elena Nikolaevna?"

She stopped and did not reply at once—not because she was angry, but because her thoughts were far away.

"No," she said at last, "I'm not angry at all."

Shubin bit his lip.

"What a preoccupied and . . . what an indifferent expression your face has . . ." he murmured.

"Elena Nikolaevna," he continued, raising his voice, "let me tell you a little story. I had a friend and this friend in his turn had a friend, who to begin with behaved like any other decent man and then, suddenly, took to drink. One day early in the morning my friend met him in the street (they weren't on close terms any more, mind you) and saw that he was drunk. So my friend could think of nothing better to do than turn his back on him. Then the other one came up to him and said, 'I wouldn't have been angry if you hadn't raised your hat to me, but why turn away? Perhaps it's grief that has driven me to this. May my ashes rest in peace.' "

Shubin remained silent.

"And is that all?" asked Elena.

"That's all."

"I don't understand you. What does it all mean? A

moment ago you were saying that I shouldn't look your way."

"Yes, and now I have told you how wicked it is to turn away."

"But I didn't . . ." Elena began.

"Didn't you?"

Elena flushed and gave Shubin her hand. He pressed it tightly.

"You think you've caught me nursing a grievance," Elena said, "but your suspicion is unjustified. I wasn't avoiding you at all."

"Let's agree that you weren't. But admit that you have a thousand thoughts in your head at the moment, not one of which you would confide to me. Aren't I right?"

"Perhaps you are."

"But why is this? Why?"

"They are not very clear even to myself," murmured Elena.

"That's precisely why you should confide them to somebody," Shubin went on, "but I'll tell you the real reason why. You've a bad opinion of me."

"Have I?"

"Yes, you have. You believe that because I'm an artist, almost everything in me is put on, that not only am I incapable of any work—in this you're probably right—but incapable, too, of any real depth of feeling, that even my tears are insincere, that I'm a gossip and a chatterbox—and all this merely because I'm an artist. Are we really such wretched, God-forsaken people? I could swear that you do not even believe in my remorse."

"No, Pavel Jakovlevich, I do believe in your remorse

and also in your tears, but I can't help thinking that you find entertainment in both.''

Shubin gave a start. ''Yes, I see now that this is what the doctors call an incurable case, *casus incurabilis*. There's nothing left but to bow one's head in resignation. But heavens alive, is it really true that I'm so busy playing a part when there is a heart like yours beating at my side? When I know that I shall never penetrate that heart, never know why it is sad, or why it is merry, what it longs for and what it broods about, or whither it is going? Tell me,'' he murmured after a short pause, ''you would never, under any circumstances, fall in love with an artist, would you?''

Elena looked him straight in the eyes. ''I don't think I would, Pavel Jakovlevich.''

''Q.E.D.,'' murmured Shubin with comic desperation. ''After this, I suppose it would be more seemly for me not to interfere with your solitary walk. A professor would have asked you: 'What premises caused you to say that you would not?' But I'm not a professor, I'm a child according to you and don't forget that one should not turn one's back on a child. Good-bye. May my ashes rest in peace.''

Elena was on the point of stopping him, but after a moment's consideration repeated after him, ''Good-bye.''

Shubin left the grounds. Not far from the Stakhov villa he met Bersenev. He was walking swiftly, his head bent down, his hat pushed backwards.

''Andrei Petrovich!'' Shubin shouted.

Bersenev stopped.

''Go on, go on.'' continued Shubin, ''I was just calling out, I didn't mean to stop you—and go straight to the garden where you will find Elena. I believe she's waiting for you. . . . Anyway, she's waiting for somebody. Do you appreciate the force of that remark? She is *waiting*! You know, my boy, the astonishing thing is that I've been living in the same house with her for two years, that I have been in love with her, but it's only just now, at this very moment, that I—I wouldn't say understood her—but saw her for the first time. Saw her and spread out my hands in wonder. Don't look at me, please, with such a malicious smile. It doesn't suit your serious face. I know you wish to remind me about Annushka. Well, what about it? I'm not denying it. The Annushkas are the ones for us. So long live the Annushkas and the Zoës, and even the Augustina Khristianovnas! You go and meet Elena now, and I'll find my way . . . to Annushka, you think? No, my boy, worse than that: to Prince Chikurassov. There is such a person—a patron of the arts, a Tartar from Kazan, a kind of Volgin. See this invitation card with the letters R.S.V.P.? I get no peace, not even in the country! Addio!''

Bersenev listened to Shubin's tirade in silence, and felt slightly embarrassed on his account. He then walked on towards the Stakhov villa, while Shubin did in fact drive over to Prince Chikurassov's, where he behaved with the most pointed impudence, though with perfect politeness. The Tartar from Kazan, the patron of the arts, roared with laughter, so did his guests, but nobody enjoyed himself and everyone felt annoyed with each other on leaving. In the same way, two men, only slightly acquainted with each other, might meet on the Nevsky Prospect, suddenly bare their teeth and screw up their eyes, nose and cheeks into an artificial smile, and as soon as they have passed one another resume the indifferent or sullen expression of a sufferer from the piles.

# CHAPTER X

ELENA—SHE WAS not in the garden any more, but in the sitting-room—greeted Bersenev with great friendliness and immediately, indeed almost impatiently, picked up the threads of the previous day's conversation. She was alone. Nikolai Artemievich had disappeared somewhere on the sly. Anna Vassilievna was lying upstairs with a wet towel round her head. Zoë sat at her side, her skirts carefully spread out and her hands folded in her lap. Uvar Ivanovich was resting in the attic on a broad and comfortable couch which had been christened "The Autosleep". Bersenev returned to the subject of his father, whose memory he held in high esteem. Let us, too, say a few words about him. The owner of eighty-two "souls"* whom he had freed before his death, a member of the Illuminati,† an old Göttingen student, author of a manuscript entitled *Manifestations or Revelations of Spirit in the World* (a work in which the influence of Schelling, Swedenborg and republican ideas were jumbled together in the most peculiar manner), Bersenev's father had brought him to Moscow as a small boy, directly after his mother's death, and had himself taken his education in hand. He prepared every lesson beforehand, worked very

* Serfs.—*Translator's note.*

† A secret religious and political society in Europe in the middle of the eighteenth century.—*Translator's note.*

conscientiously and quite unsuccessfully; he was a dreamer, a mystic, a bookworm, spoke with a stammer in a hoarse voice, used elaborate and obscure expressions, mostly metaphors, and was shy even of his son, to whom he was passionately devoted. No wonder that his son merely fluttered his eyelids during lessons and failed to make the slightest progress. The old man (he was almost fifty, having married very late) at last realized that it was a failure and sent his Andriusha to a boarding-school. Andriusha began to study, but did not escape his parent's control; his father visited him constantly, pestering the headmaster with his suggestions and advice. The teachers, too, grew tired of the unwelcome guest who kept bringing them what they took to be all-too-profound treatises on education. Even the pupils were embarrassed by the sight of the old man's swarthy, pock-marked face and his gaunt figure, always clad in a flapping tail-coat. They never suspected then that the heart of the sullen gentleman who never smiled, who had a long nose and walked like a crane, ached for each one of them almost as much as for his own son. One day, it suddenly occurred to him to speak to them about George Washington: "Boys!" he roared, but at the first sound of his strange voice the boys ran away. Life was no bed of roses for the honest student from Göttingen. The historical process constantly defeated him; he stumbled under the burden of question and conjecture. When young Bersenev went to the University, he accompanied him to the lectures, but his health began to fail him. The events of '48 undermined him completely (his whole book would need to be rewritten) and he died in the winter of 1853, before his son had finished at the University, but rejoicing with him in anticipation of his success in his finals and giving his blessing to his son's future service to science. "I'm passing on the torch to you," he said to him two hours before he died. "I held it up as long as I could, don't let it drop from your hand until the end."

Bersenev spoke to Elena for a long time about his father. The embarrassment he had felt in her presence had vanished and with it his lisp. They broached the subject of the University.

"Tell me", asked Elena, "were there any remarkable people among your fellow-students?"

Bersenev recalled Shubin's words. "No, Elena Nikolaevna, to tell you the truth, there was not one remarkable man among us. None, indeed! They say that Moscow University has seen great days in the past. But not now. It is merely a school at present, not a university. I found it hard to get on with my fellow-students," he added, lowering his voice.

"Hard?" murmured Elena.

"I must make one exception, however," Bersenev went on. "I know one student, not of my year, it is true, but a truly remarkable man."

"What is his name?" Elena promptly asked.

"Insarov, Dmitri Nikanorich. He's a Bulgarian. . . ."

"Not Russian?"

"No."

"Why does he live in Moscow then?"

"He came to study. And do you know why he is studying? He has only one aim: the liberation of his country. He has had an unusual career. His father was a well-to-do merchant from Tirnov. Tirnov is now a small town, but when Bulgaria was an independent kingdom, it was the capital. He traded in Sofia, had contacts with Russia—his sister, Insarov's aunt, still lives in Kiev, married to a history teacher in a local school. In 1835, that is eighteen years ago, a terrible crime was committed: Insarov's mother suddenly disappeared without a trace, and a week later was found murdered."

Elena shuddered. Bersenev stopped.

"Go on, go on," she said.

"There were rumours that a Turkish Aga had captured her and killed her. Her husband, Insarov's father, having discovered the truth, wanted to have his revenge, but he only wounded the murderer with his dagger. He was shot."

"Shot? Without trial?"

"Yes. Insarov at that time was not yet eight years old. He was taken care of by some neighbours. His aunt heard about what had happened to her brother's family and wished to have her nephew with her. He was taken first to Odessa, then to Kiev, where he lived for twelve years. That's why he speaks such good Russian."

"He speaks Russian?"

"Like you and me. When he was twenty (at the beginning of 1848) he felt a longing to return to his own country. He went to Sofia, to Tirnov, tramped over the whole of Bulgaria for two years and once again learnt his native language. The Turkish Government was pursuing him and he probably had to face many dangers in the course of those two years. I saw a large scar on his neck one day, probably an old wound; but he doesn't like to raise that subject. He is also, in his way, a taciturn person. I've tried to question him: it's no use, though. He answers with commonplaces. He's terribly stubborn. In 1850, he came back to Russia, to Moscow, with the sole object of finishing his studies, getting in closer touch with the Russians, and then, when he leaves the University . . ."

"Then what?" interrupted Elena.

"God will provide. It's hard to foresee."

Elena kept her eyes fixed on Bersenev. "You've aroused my curiosity with your story," she murmured, "What is he like, your—what did you say his name was—Insarov?"

"How should I describe him . . .? In my opinion he's not bad-looking, but you'll be able to judge for yourself."

"How?"

"I'll bring him to see you. He's moving to our village and is going to live in my house."

"Really! But will he want to come and see us?"

"Of course he will. He'll be delighted."

"He isn't proud?"

"Proud? Not he. Or, if you like, he *is* proud, but not in the sense you mean. He will, for instance, never borrow money from anyone."

"Is he poor?"

"Yes, he certainly isn't rich. He collected the little that was left of his father's fortune when he went to Bulgaria and his aunt helps him now and then, but all told it amounts to very little      "

"He must be a man of great character," remarked Elena.

"Yes, he has a will of iron. At the same time—you will see it for yourself—there is something childlike and open about him in spite of his determination and reserve. It is true that his frankness is not *our* paltry frankness—the frankness of people who have actually nothing to conceal . . . . Well, anyway, I'll bring him and show him to you."

"He isn't shy?" Elena asked again.

61

"No, he isn't shy. Only conceited people are shy."

"Are you conceited then?"

Bersenev felt embarrassed and spread out his hands in perplexity.

"You really have made me curious," went on Elena. "Tell me, didn't he have his revenge on the Turkish Aga?"

Bersenev smiled. "Revenge only happens in novels, Elena Nikolaevna. Besides, in these twelve years the Turkish Aga may have died."

"But Mr. Insarov didn't say anything about it to you?"

"No, he didn't."

"Why did he go to Sofia?"

"His father had lived there."

Elena grew thoughtful. "To free one's country . . ." she murmured. "It gives one a feeling of awe merely to utter those words—they're so great and noble. . . ."

At that moment, Anna Vassilievna walked into the room and the conversation stopped. Strange emotions rose in Bersenev's heart as he made his way home that evening. He did not regret his intention of bringing Elena and Insarov together. It seemed to him that the deep interest he had aroused in her by his stories about the young Bulgarian was perfectly natural—hadn't he himself tried to kindle it? But there was a dark and secret thought lurking at the back of his mind, something ominous in the sadness he felt. It did not prevent him, however, from picking up the *History of the Hohenstaufens* and starting to read again from the page where he had left off the day before.

# CHAPTER XI

TWO DAYS LATER, according to plan, Insarov arrived with his belongings at Bersenev's house. He had no servant with him, but he tidied up his room himself, arranged the furniture, wiped away the dust and swept the floor. He had a good deal of trouble with his writing-desk which refused to fit into the recess allotted to it; in the end, however, with the silent determination that was characteristic of him, he managed to get it in. Having settled down, he asked Bersenev to take ten roubles from him on account and, armed with a walking stick, proceeded to inspect the neighbourhood of his new home. He came back about three hours later and, to Bersenev's invitation to share his meal with him, replied that he would agree to do so to-day, but that he had already made arrangements with the housekeeper and would in future get his food from her.

"But why?" exclaimed Bersenev, "you'll only be badly fed if you do. The woman can't cook at all. Why not have your meals with me and we could share the expense?"

"I can't afford to spend as much money on food as you do," Insarov replied with a quiet smile.

There was something in that smile that made it impossible to insist. Bersenev said nothing more. After dinner, he offered to take him to the Stakhovs, but Insarov replied that he had planned to devote the whole evening to correspondence with his compatriots and therefore would be glad if the visit to the Stakhovs could be postponed to another day. Bersenev already knew how inexorable insarov could be in his decisions, but it was only now, living with him under the same roof, that he fully realized that it was as impossible to make him change his plans, as it was to prevent his keeping a promise. Being essentially Russian, Bersenev was apt at first to consider such more-than-German meticulousness as inhuman, even a little ridiculous, but he soon got used to it and finally decided that it was, if not positively estimable, at any rate extremely convenient.

The second day after his arrival, Insarov got up at 4 a.m., made a brisk tour of Kunzovo, bathed in the river, drank a glass of cold milk and settled down to work. He certainly had enough work on his hands: he was studying Russian history, law and political economy; translating Bulgarian songs and memoirs; collecting material on the Eastern question; compiling a Bulgarian grammar for Russians and a Russian one for Bulgarians.

Bersenev came to his room and they talked about Feuerbach; Insarov listened to him attentively, argued little but to the point. One could see from his arguments that he was trying to find out for himself whether it was essential for him to study Feuerbach, or whether he could get on without him. Bersenev turned the conversation to the subject of his work and asked whether he could be shown some of it. Insarov read him his translation of two or three Bulgarian songs and wanted to know his opinion of it. Bersenev thought the translation correct but not spirited enough. Insarov made a note of this criticism. The songs led Bersenev on to the present situation in Bulgaria and here he noticed for the first time the change that took place in Insarov at the mere mention of his country. It wasn't that his face flushed, or that his voice became more strident—no, it was as if his whole being suddenly asserted itself, grew firmer, strained forward; the outline of his lips became more defined and implacable; and a sombre but unquenchable fire flared up in the depth of his eyes. Insarov was not disposed to enlarge upon his own trip to his country, but he was ready to speak to anyone about Bulgaria in general. He talked with deliberation about the Turks, about their measures of oppression, about the misery and need of his countrymen, of their hopes; in every word one was aware of the thoughtful concentration of a single, long-standing passion.

"Who knows?" Bersenev thought to himself as he listened, "maybe he did have his revenge on the Aga after all?"

Insarov was still talking, when the door opened and Shubin appeared on the threshold. He strolled into the room in a rather too affable and nonchalant manner; Bersenev, who knew him well, realized at once that something was jarring on him.

"I'll introduce myself without ceremony," he began with an innocent and open expression on his face. "My name's Shubin, I'm a friend of that young man over there (he pointed to Bersenev). You're Mr. Insarov, aren't you?"

"I am."

"Let's shake hands then, and be friends. I don't know if Bersenev has spoken to you about me. He's certainly told me a lot about you. So you live here? That's splendid! Don't mind my staring at you like this. I'm a sculptor by profession and I see that I shall soon be asking you for permission to model your head.''

''My head is at your service,'' murmured Insarov.

''What shall we do to-day, eh?'' continued Shubin, suddenly sitting down on a low chair and planting both hands on his open knees. ''Andrei Petrovich, has your honour got any plan for the coming day? The weather's fine, there's such a delicious smell of hay and wild strawberry in the air . . . it's as if one were drinking an infusion. We must hatch a bright idea of sorts. Let's show the new inhabitant of Kunzovo all its numerous beauty-spots.'' (There's something jarring on him, Bersenev went on thinking to himself.) ''Why don't you speak, friend Horatio? Let wisdom fall from your lips. Shall we set our wits to devise a plan or not?''

''I don't know about Insarov,'' remarked Bersenev, ''he seems to be planning to work.''

Shubin turned in his chair. ''You intend to work?'' he asked through his nose.

''No,'' Insarov replied, ''I can devote the day to a walk.''

''Ah!'' exclaimed Shubin, ''that's all right, then. Go, my dear Andrei Petrovich, cover your wise head with a hat, and let us start at random and let our feet take us where they will. Our feet are young, they will carry us far. I know a nasty little inn where they'll give us a foul meal, but we'll have lots of fun. Let's go.''

Half an hour later they were all walking along the Moscow river. Insarov wore a strange flapping cap which provoked Shubin's somewhat exaggerated admiration. He walked in a leisurely way, gazed right and left, breathed deeply, talked and smiled contentedly—he had decided to devote the day to pleasure and was fully enjoying it.

"Good little boys go for walks like this on Sundays," Shubin whispered to Bersenev.

Shubin, on the other hand, was playing the fool, rushing on ahead, posing in the attitudes of well-known statues, turning somersaults on the grass. Insarov's calm did not exactly irritate him, but it made him show off.

"What's all the affectation for, Froggy?" Bersenev said to him once or twice.

"Yes, I'm French—half French," Shubin retorted, "and you'd do well to keep the golden mean between being playful and solemn, as a waiter once said to me."

The young men turned away from the river and walked along a deep and narrow passage between two walls of tall golden corn. A bluish shadow fell on them from one of these walls—the rays of the sun seemed to flit over the tops of the stalks. The skylarks were singing, the quails piping, the green grass shimmering; a warm breeze stirred, lifting the stems and swaying the blooms of the flowers. After much rambling about and resting and chattering (Shubin even tried to play leap-frog with a small toothless vagabond, who kept on laughing—no matter what the "gents" might or might not do to him)—the young men reached the "nasty" little inn. The servant almost knocked them all sideways in his zeal and in fact served them with a perfectly foul meal, washed down with some Eastern wine, which did not, however, prevent them, as Shubin had foretold, from enjoying themselves immensely. Shubin, though he made the most noise about it, enjoyed himself the least of the three. He drank the health of the "misunderstood" but celebrated Venelin*

* Bulgarian scientist and fighter for independence.—*Translator's note.*

and the health of the Bulgarian Prince Krum, Khrum or Khrom, who had lived "almost as far back as Adam".

"In the ninth century," Insarov corrected him.

"In the ninth?" exclaimed Shubin, "Oh, what bliss!"

Bersenev noticed that all the time Shubin was showing off, playing the fool, and joking, he was evidently cross-examining Insarov, studying him with ill-concealed excitement, while Insarov remained tranquil and serene. Finally, they returned home, changed, and in order to carry on in the same way as they had chosen to begin the day, decided to go and visit the Stakhovs the same evening. Shubin went on ahead to herald their arrival.

## CHAPTER XII

"OUR HERO INSAROV is going to grace us with his presence in a moment," Shubin solemnly announced, walking into the Stakhovs' sitting-room, where Zoë and Elena were alone at the time.

"Wer?" Zoë asked in German. When taken by surprise, she always used her mother tongue. Elena straightened herself. Shubin glanced at her with a simpering smile. It annoyed her, but she said nothing.

"Did you hear what I said?" he repeated. "Mr. Insarov is on his way here."

"I heard you," she replied, "and I also heard what you called him. I must say you surprise me. Before Mr. Insarov has even crossed the threshold, you're already up to your tricks."

Shubin was suddenly disconcerted. "You're right, you're always right, Elena Nikolaevna," he mumbled, "I swear I was only joking. . . . He and I have spent the whole day out walking and he's a splendid fellow, I assure you."

"I wasn't asking you about that," Elena murmured.

"Is Mr. Insarov young?" asked Zoë.

"He is one hundred and forty-four years old," replied Shubin irritably.

The pageboy announced the arrival of the two friends. They came in. Bersenev introduced Insarov. Elena asked them to sit down and sat down herself, while Zoë went upstairs to tell Anna Vassilievna. The conversation began insignificantly, like all opening conversations. Shubin looked on silently from his corner, but there was nothing to observe. He noticed in Elena a trace of her suppressed irritation with himself—that was all. He gazed at Bersenev and Insarov and, as a sculptor, compared their faces. Neither of them, he thought to himself, is handsome; the Bulgarian's face is full of character, statuesque—at the moment it's in a good light. The Russian's lends itself more to painting—no lines, only expression. One could fall in love with either, though. She is not yet in love with Bersenev, he decided, but she will be.

Anna Vassilievna appeared in the drawing-room and they began talking, not as people usually do in country houses, but as though they were there only for the summer. It was an extremely varied conversation as regards the number of subjects discussed, but it was interrupted every few minutes by short and rather painful silences. During one of them, Anna Vassilievna turned to Zoë. Shubin knew what this meant and pulled a long face. Meanwhile, Zoë went over to the piano and played and sang her little pieces.

Uvar Ivanovich made a move to emerge from behind the door, but having twiddled his fingers, beat a retreat. Tea was then served, and afterwards the whole company strolled round the garden. Darkness fell and the guests departed.

Insarov actually produced less impression on Elena than she had expected—or, to be more precise, he produced a different impression to the one she expected. She liked his straightforward, easy manner—she also liked his face;

but his personality, as a whole, calm, firm and common-place, somehow did not correspond to the picture she had formed in her mind on the strength of Bersenev's stories. Without being aware of it she had expected something more fateful. "It's true he didn't speak much to-day," she thought. "I'm to blame for that. I didn't draw him out. Let's wait till next time. But his eyes are full of expression and they're honest eyes." She felt that what she really wanted was not to bow down in admiration before him, but to stretch out a friendly hand, and this perplexed her —she had imagined heroes, people like Insarov, quite different to this man. The word "hero" reminded her of Shubin, and lying now in bed, she flushed with anger.

"How did you like your new friends?" Bersenev asked Insarov on the way back.

"Very much indeed," replied Insarov. "Particularly the daughter. She must be a very fine young woman. She gets excited easily and it is the right kind of excitement."

"We must go and see them often," remarked Bersenev.

"Yes, we must," murmured Insarov and did not utter another word all the rest of the way. He shut himself up in his room at once, but his candle was still burning long after midnight.

Bersenev had not had time to read a chapter of Raumer's book, when a handful of fine gravel was flung at his window and rattled against the pane. He could not help starting; he opened the window and saw Shubin, white as a sheet.

"You *are* a restless creature, you night-bird," began Bersenev.

"Sh—sh . . ." Shubin interrupted him. "I've come

to you in secret, like Max to Agatha.* I simply must tell you something very private."

"Well, come to my room."

"No, I won't," Shubin retorted and leant against the window-sill. "It's much more fun this way, it has a Spanish air about it. First of all, my heartiest congratulations—your shares have gone up. Your reputed wonder-man has been a sad fiasco. I can give you my word for it. And to prove my objectivity, listen to me; here is a list of Mr. Insarov's chief peculiarities. No talents, poetic sense nil, working capacity unlimited, a good memory, a not too versatile or profound intelligence, but a lively and solid one; he's crisp and forceful and even eloquent when you touch upon the question of his (between ourselves) boring old Bulgaria. You'll say I'm being unfair? Another point: you'll never be on familiar terms with him; no one ever has been. I, as an artist, am repulsive to him, and I'm proud of it. Dry, dry as sand, and capable of grinding us all to dust. He's bound up with his country, not like our empty vessels who fawn on the people, begging—'Oh, waters of life, pour into us!' His task is an easier one, it is true, easier to grasp—all that has to be done is turn out the Turks—as though there was much in that! But all these qualities, thank God, don't attract women. No appeal, no charm about him as there is about you and me."

"I don't see what I have to do with it," muttered Bersenev, "and you're mistaken about the rest, too. You aren't at all repulsive to him and he's on familiar terms with his countrymen, I know for a fact. . . ."

"That's quite another matter! For them he's a hero,

* Characters from Weber's opera *Der Freischütz.—Translator's note.*

72

but to tell you the truth, my idea of a hero is quite different: a hero should not be able to speak, he should roar like a bull, and when he butts with his horns, walls should come tumbling down. And he shouldn't know either why he butts them, but merely that he does. Possibly in our time, though, there's a demand for heroes of a different calibre."

"Why this preoccupation with Insarov?" asked Bersenev. "Did you really come all the way here just to give me an account of his character?"

"I came here," began Shubin, "because I felt very depressed at home."

"I see. Are you going to burst into tears again?"

"You may well laugh! I've come because I could kick myself, because I'm consumed by despair, vexation and jealousy. . . ."

"Jealousy? Of whom?"

"Of you, of him, of everyone. It's maddening to think that if I'd understood her before, if I'd been more skilful in my approach. . . . But what's the use of talking about it! It'll end by my continuing my jokes and pranks and antics, as she calls them—and then, the noose."

"Oh, no, there'll be no noose for you," remarked Bersenev.

"Not on a night like this, of course; but wait till the autumn comes. On a night like this people may of course die, but only of happiness. Ah, happiness! Every shadow thrown by the trees across the road seems to be whispering now: 'I know where happiness lies; shall I tell you?' I'd suggest that you come out for a walk, but I can see you're too much under Insarov's prosaic influence. Go to sleep and dream of mathematical problems, while my heart is breaking. When you and your sort see a fellow laughing, you think he must be happy; you can prove to him that he's a humbug and that consequently he can't be suffering. . . . You and your sort! May God forgive you!"

Shubin walked quickly away from the window.

"Annushka!" Bersenev was on the point of shouting after him, but refrained. Shubin had really looked desperate. Indeed a few moments later Bersenev imagined he heard sobbing. He got up and opened the window, but all was still; only in the distance someone—a passing peasant probably—was humming "The Steppe of Mozdok".

# CHAPTER XIII

DURING THE FIRST fortnight following Insarov's arrival in the neighbourhood of Kunzovo, he did not visit the Stakhovs more than four or five times; Bersenev went there every other day. Elena was always glad to see him. Their conversation was always lively and interesting; yet he often came home with a sad expression on his face. Shubin was hardly ever visible; he was feverishly engrossed with his sculpture, either shut up in his room, from which he emerged from time to time in a blouse smeared all over with clay, or spent his days in Moscow where he had a studio and where his models, his friends, Italian casters, and teachers came to see him.

Elena had not once had the opportunity of talking to Insarov as she would have liked to do; when he was not there she planned to ask him about so many things, but when he arrived she felt ashamed of the preparations she had made. Insarov's very tranquillity embarrassed her; it seemed to her that she had no right to draw him out and she determined to wait. She felt, however, that with every visit, insignificant as the words they exchanged may have been, he attracted her more and more, but somehow it happened that they were never left alone and one must have at least a few moments alone with someone before any degree of intimacy can be established.

She talked a lot about him with Bersenev. Bersenev

realized that Insarov had captured Elena's imagination and was glad that his friend had not turned out to be the "sad fiasco" of Shubin's description. He told her with great enthusiasm and down to the smallest detail all he knew about him—(it often happens that when we want to curry favour with someone, we sing the praises of our friends, never suspecting that in doing so we are praising ourselves)—and only from time to time, when Elena's pale cheeks became slightly flushed and her look more limpid and wide-eyed, did the envious sadness, which he had already experienced before, tug at his heart.

One day Bersenev arrived at the Stakhovs, not at his usual hour, but shortly after ten in the morning. Elena came out into the hall to meet him.

"You'll be surprised to hear," he began with a strained smile, "that our Insarov has disappeared."

"Disappeared?" asked Elena.

"Yes. Two days ago he went away in the evening, and hasn't been back since."

"He didn't tell you where he was going?"

"No."

Elena sank into a chair. "He's probably gone to Moscow," she murmured, trying to appear indifferent and at the same time surprised at herself for trying to appear so.

"I don't think so," said Bersenev; "he didn't go alone."

"Who with?"

"Two days ago, just before dinner, two men came to see him, fellow countrymen of his, presumably."

"Bulgarians? What makes you think that?"

"Because as far as I could make out they were talking to him in a language I didn't know, although I could

76

recognize it as Slavonic. Elena Nikolaevna, you're always saying that there is little mystery about Insarov—but what could have been more mysterious than that visit? Imagine it: they walked into his room and at once began shouting and arguing, so fiercely, so savagely. He shouted, too."

"He shouted?"

"Yes, he did. He shouted at them. They seemed to be accusing one another. If only you'd seen these visitors! Their flat swarthy faces and their broad cheek-bones, their hawk-like noses; over forty, both of them. They were poorly dressed, sweaty and grimy—not really work-men, and yet not gentlemen—heaven alone knows who they were."

"And he went away with them?"

"Yes. He gave them something to eat and went off with them. The landlady told me that between them they emptied a huge pot of gruel. She said they gulped it down like wolves, seeing who would finish first."

Elena smiled faintly. "You'll see that it will all have a very prosaic explanation," she murmured.

"Pray God it will! But you shouldn't have used the word prosaic. There's nothing prosaic about Insarov, whatever Shubin may say."

"Shubin!" interrupted Elena and shrugged her shoulders. "But you must admit that those two gentlemen gulping down their gruel. . . ."

"Even Themistocles had to eat before the battle of Salamis," Bersenev remarked with a smile.

"Yes, but then the battle did take place the next day. Anyhow, do let me know when he comes back," added Elena, and tried to change the conversation—but some-how it didn't come off. Zoë appeared and walked about the room on tiptoe, indicating that Anna Vassilievna was still asleep.

Bersenev went away.

During the evening of the same day, a note came from him for Elena. "He has returned," he wrote, "very sunburnt and covered with dust up to the eyebrows—but I haven't found out where he's been or why—won't you try?"

"Find out!" whispered Elena to herself. "As if he would confide in me!"

## CHAPTER XIV

THE NEXT AFTERNOON, about two o'clock, Elena was standing in the garden in front of a small shed, where she kept two mongrel puppies. (The gardener had found them abandoned under a hedge and had brought them to his young mistress, the laundry-woman having told him that she loved all kinds of animals. He was not mistaken in his expectations; Elena gave him a quarter of a rouble.) She peered into the shed to make sure that the puppies were alive and well and had been given a fresh layer of straw, and when she turned round, she very nearly cried out, for Insarov was walking towards her along the path.

"Good-morning," he said, coming closer and taking off his cap. She noticed that he had, indeed, got very sunburnt in the last three days. "I wanted to come with Andrei Petrovich, but he was dawdling about, so I made my way alone. There is no one to be seen in your house, everybody either asleep or out, so I came here."

"You seem to be apologizing," replied Elena, "there's no need to do that—we are always glad to see you. . . . Let's sit on the bench here in the shade." She sat down. Insarov took a seat beside her. 'You've been away lately, I believe?" she began.

"Yes," he replied, "I have. Did Andrei Petrovich tell you?"

Insarov glanced at her, smiled and began to play with

his cap. When he smiled he blinked rapidly with his eyes and pursed up his lips, which gave him a good-natured look.

"Andrei Petrovich probably also told you that I'd gone with some . . . disreputable-looking people," he said, continuing to smile.

Elena was slightly embarrassed, but instantly realized that with Insarov one should always speak the truth.

"Yes," she said in a firm voice.

"And what did you think of me then?" he suddenly asked her.

Elena looked up at him. "I thought then," she murmured, "that you always know what you're doing and that you're incapable of doing wrong."

"Thank you for that. You see, Elena Nikolaevna," he began, trustfully moving closer to her, "there's only a small group of us here, some of them half-educated people, but all deeply devoted to the common cause. Unfortunately, one can't avoid quarrels and they all know me and trust me, so they came and asked me to straighten out a small dispute. So I went."

"Was it far from here?"

"I had to go nearly forty-five miles—to the Troitzki Monastery. Some of our people also live there near the Monastery. Anyway, I didn't go in vain. The quarrel was settled."

"Was it difficult?"

"It was. One of them was very obstinate. Refused to give back the money."

"What, it was about money?"

"Yes, and a small sum at that. What did you think it was?"

"And you went as far as forty-five miles for such a trifle? Wasted three days!"

"It's not a trifle, Elena Nikolaevna, when one's country-men are mixed up in it. It would have been a sin to refuse. Look at yourself—I can see that you don't refuse help even to a puppy and I can only admire you for it. And as far as wasting my time is concerned, there's no great harm in that. I'll catch up with it. Our time doesn't belong to us."

"To whom, then, does it belong?"

"To anyone who needs it. I've told you all about this on the spur of the moment because I value your opinion. I can well imagine how Andrei Petrovich's story must have surprised you!"

"You value my opinion?" Elena whispered. "Why?"

Insarov smiled again. "Because you're a nice young woman, not one of those aristocrats . . . that's why."

There was a slight pause.

"Dmitri Nikanorich," said Elena, "you know that this is the first time that you've been so frank with me."

"Is it really? It seems to me that I've always said to you what came into my mind."

"No, this is the first time and it makes me very happy. I also want to be quite frank with you. May I?"

Insarov laughed, saying, "Yes, you may."

"I warn you that I'm very inquisitive."

"Never mind, go on."

"Andrei Petrovich told me a lot about your life, your young days. I know of the tragedy . . . the dreadful tragedy. . . . I know that you went back to your country after that. . . . Don't answer me, for God's sake, don't answer if my question seems indiscreet . . . but there's one thought that torments me. . . . Tell me, did you ever see the man again? . . ." Elena caught her breath. She was both ashamed and afraid of her own boldness. Insarov looked at her intently, his eyes half shut, stroking his chin with his fingers.

"Elena Nikolaevna," he began at last—his voice was lower than usual and this almost frightened Elena. "I know whom you mean by that man. No, I didn't come across him, thank God! I didn't look for him. I didn't look for him, not because I didn't consider myself entitled to kill him—I would kill him quite calmly—but because this is no time for personal revenge when our concern is a general, a national revenge—no, revenge is not the right word—when our concern is the liberation of a nation. The one thing would have got in the way of the other. The time will come for the other one as well—it will come," he repeated, shaking his head.

Elena gave him a sidelong glance. "You love your country very much?" she said timidly.

"That remains to be seen," he replied. "When a person dies for his country, then you can say that he loves it."

"So that if you were prevented from returning to Bulgaria," continued Elena, "you would find it very hard to live in Russia?"

Insarov lowered his eyes. "I don't think I should be able to bear it," he murmured.

"Tell me," Elena went on, "is it very difficult to learn Bulgarian?"

"Not at all. A Russian ought to be ashamed not to know Bulgarian. A Russian ought to know all the Slavonic languages. Would you like me to bring you some Bulgarian books? You will see how easy it is. What songs we have—

no worse than the Serbian ones! Let me try and translate one for you. It's a song about . . . but do you know anything of our history?"

"No, I know nothing about it," replied Elena.

"Well, let me bring you a book. You will learn at least the chief facts about it. But now, do listen to the song, or would it be better if I brought you the written translation? I'm sure that you will learn to love us—you, who love all the oppressed. . . . If only you knew what a beautiful country ours is! But it is down-trodden and tortured," he went on, unable to restrain a movement of his hand, and his face darkened. "Everything has been taken away from us, our churches, our rights, our land. The cursed Turks herd us like cattle, butcher us!"

"Dmitri Nikanorich!" exclaimed Elena.

He stopped. "Forgive me. I can't speak calmly about it. But you asked me just now whether I love my country. What else is there to love on this earth? What else is there that is permanent, above suspicion, in which one can have faith, as one has faith in God? And when this country needs you. . . . And mind you, the last peasant, the last beggar in Bulgaria wants the same things that I do. We all have the same aim. You realize what strength and assurance this can give."

Insarov broke off for a moment and then went on again about Bulgaria. Elena listened to him with deep, absorbed, and sorrowful attention. When he had finished she asked once more, "So nothing could make you stay in Russia?"

And when he went away, she followed him for a long time with her eyes. That day he became a different person for her. When she saw him go, it was a different man from the one she had seen arrive two hours before. From that day his visits became more frequent and Bersenev's more rare. Something strange, of which they were both aware, stood between the two friends, something they could not give a name to and were afraid to bring into the open.

A month passed in this way.

# CHAPTER XV

ANNA VASSILIEVNA, AS the reader already knows, liked to stay at home, but sometimes, quite unexpectedly, she developed an uncontrollable longing for something unusual, for a wonderful *partie de plaisir*, and the more elaborate this *partie de plaisir*, the more it involved preparations and planning, the more excited she was, and the more pleased. If this paroxysm overcame her in the winter, she gave instructions for two or three boxes to be reserved all in a row, invited all her friends and took them to the theatre or even to a *bal masqué*; in the summer she would go as far out of town as possible. The next day she would complain of a headache, groan and keep to her bed, but a month or so later the craving for the "unusual" would overcome her again. This is what happened now: somebody mentioned in her presence the beauties of Tsaritsin and Anna Vassilievna suddenly declared that she was leaving for Tsaritsin the day after next. The house was thrown into a state of uproar, a messenger was sent to Moscow to fetch Nikolai Artemievich; the butler went with him to buy wine, pâté and other delicacies; to Shubin fell the duty of hiring a phaeton (one carriage was not sufficient) and see about relays of horses; the groom went twice to Bersenev and Insarov with two invitation cards, written out by Zoë, first in Russian, then in French. Anna Vassilievna busied herself with the girls' travelling clothes. But the *partie de plaisir* almost failed to take place: Nikolai Artemievich arrived from Moscow in a sour and unsympathetic—*frondiste*—state of mind (he was sulking with Augustina Khristianovna) and upon hearing what it was all about, firmly declared that he wouldn't go, that to dash from Kunzovo to Moscow, from Moscow to Tsaritsin, and then from Tsaritsin again to Moscow and from Moscow again to Kunzovo, was absurd, and finally, he added, "if someone proves to me that one point of the globe can be more amusing than another, then I will go." No one, obviously, could prove this to his satisfaction, and Anna Vassilievna, for want of a suitable escort, was preparing to give up the outing when she remembered Uvar Ivanovich and, in her distress, sent up to his small room for him, remarking that "a drowning person would catch even at a straw". They woke him up, he came down, listened in silence to Anna Vassilievna's proposal, twiddled his fingers and, to everybody's astonishment, agreed to it. Anna Vassilievna kissed him on the cheek and called him darling. Nikolai Artemievich gave a contemptuous smile and said "quelle bourde!" (he liked throwing out "smart" French words casually) and next morning at 7 a.m. the carriage and the phaeton, packed to the brim, rolled out of the yard of the Stakhovs' villa. The ladies, the maid and Bersenev sat in the carriage, Insarov had settled himself on the box, Shubin and Uvar Ivanovich followed in the phaeton. It was Uvar Ivanovich who had made Shubin a sign with his finger inviting him to go with him. He knew that Shubin would tease him all the way, but between the "elemental force" and the young artist there existed a strange bond and a kind of cantankerous intimacy. This time, however, Shubin left his fat friend in peace; he was silent, absent-minded and in a mellow mood.

The sun already stood high in the cloudless blue sky when the carriages rolled up to the ruins of the Tsaritsin castle, sinister and dismal even at midday. The whole company got out on to the grass and went straight to the garden. Elena and Zoë walked in front with Insarov; behind them, with an expression of perfect bliss on her face, marched Anna Vassilievna on Uvar Ivanovich's arm. He puffed and wobbled along, his new straw hat cut into his forehead, his feet were hot in their high boots, and yet he, too, looked happy. Shubin and Bersenev brought up the rear of the procession.

"We'll be in the reserve, like old veterans, my boy," Shubin whispered to Bersenev, "Bulgaria is in the van," he added, indicating Elena with his eyebrows.

The weather was perfect. Everything around blossomed and hummed and sang; the surface of the lakes shimmered in the distance; everyone felt festive and serene. "Ah, how wonderful, how wonderful," Anna Vassilievna kept on repeating. Uvar Ivanovich nodded his head approvingly in reply to her ecstatic exclamations and once even murmured, "There's no denying it."

Elena occasionally exchanged a word with Insarov. Zoë held the edge of her broad hat with two small fingers and coquettishly displayed her small feet in their pale grey, blunt-toed shoes under a pink light woollen frock, and glanced now to right or left, now behind her.

"Aha!" Shubin suddenly exclaimed in an undertone, "Zoë Nikitishna's looking back over her shoulder. I think I'll join her. Elena Nikolaevna despises me now, as much as she respects you, Andrei Petrovich—it comes to the same thing. I'll go, I've done enough mooning. As for you, my friend, I'd advise you to turn your attention to botany; in your position it's the best thing you can do—and quite useful from the educational point of view—good-bye!" Shubin rushed up to Zoë, offered her his arm like a hoop, said, "*Ihre Hand*, Madame," clutched at her and clashed on ahead. Elena stopped, called Bersenev, and also took his arm, but went on talking to Insarov. She was asking him the Bulgarian for lily-of-the-valley, oak-tree, lime-tree, maple. (Bulgaria before everything, thought poor Andrei Petrovich to himself.)

Suddenly a cry rang out in front of them. Everybody looked up: Shubin's cigar-case was flying out of Zoë's hand into the bushes. "Wait till I have my revenge!" he shouted. He scrambled into the bushes, found the cigar-case and was returning to Zoë's side, but had hardly reached her when the cigar-case was again flying across the path. This prank was repeated at least five times, with Shubin roaring with laughter and threatening, and Zoë smiling demurely and simpering like a kitten. At last he caught her fingers and squeezed them so hard that she squealed, and after that kept blowing on her hand, pretending to be angry, while he hummed something into her ear.

"The young madcaps," Anna Vassilievna gaily observed to Uvar Ivanovich. He twiddled his fingers.

"Zoë Nikitishna is in good form," Bersenev said to Elena.

"And what about Shubin?" Elena replied.

Meanwhile, the whole company had reached a pavilion which was known by the name of Milovidova, and stopped to admire the view of the Tsaritsin lakes. These stretched one after the other for several miles and, behind them, dense wood formed a dark background. The green grass that covered the entire slope of the hill leading down to the largest lake gave the water a peculiarly brilliant, emerald-green hue. Nowhere, not even by the bank, was there the swelling of a wave or a curl of foam, not even a ripple passed across the even smoothness: it was as if a congealed, translucent mass of glass had settled heavily in a kind of huge font and the sky had joined it at the bottom —the fronded trees peering motionless into its transparent depths.

They contemplated the lovely view for a long time in silence. Even Shubin kept still, even Zoë was thoughtful. They all expressed a unanimous desire to go rowing in a boat. Shubin, Insarov and Bersenev ran down the green slope, racing each other. They found a large, gaily-coloured boat, discovered two boatmen and summoned the ladies. They came down, Uvar Ivanovich carefully following them. His attempts to get into the boat and settle down in it provoked much laughter.

"Look out, sir, don't drown us!" cried one of the boatmen, a young, pug-nosed fellow in an embroidered shirt.

"Now, now, you impudent puppy," mumbled Uvar Ivanovich.

The boat pushed off. The young men wanted to take the oars, but only Insarov knew how to use them. Shubin suggested that they should all sing a Russian song together, and started *Down Mother Volga*. Bersenev, Zoë and even Anna Vassilievna joined in (Insarov couldn't sing) but they all sang out of tune, and in the third verse the singers got into a muddle. Bersenev alone tried to carry on in a bass voice: "Nothing on the waves is seen," he continued, but very soon stopped in embarrassment. The boatmen winked at each other and grinned in silence.

"Well," Shubin turned to them, "you probably think that people like us can't sing?"

The young man in the embroidered shirt merely shook his head.

"You wait and see, pug-nose, we'll soon show you. Zoë Nikitishna, do sing us *Le Lac* by Niedermeyer. Stop rowing!"

The wet oars rose in the air like wings and remained there, the water dripping from them with a tinkling sound; the boat glided a little further and then stopped, making a slight curve on the water, like a swan.

Zoë evidently felt that she needed a little more encouragement.

"Allons!" Anna Vassilievna murmured to her kindly. Zoë took off her hat and began to sing.

*Oh Lac, l'année à peine a fini sa carrière....*

Her voice, small yet clear, seemed to race along the mirrored lake, every word echoing deep in the woods as though there, too, someone was mysteriously and distinctly singing, but with an unhuman, unearthly voice. When she had finished, somebody from a summer-house on the bank shouted a loud encore, and a crowd of red-faced Germans, who had come to Tsaritsin for a drinking spree, bounded out of it. Some of them were in short sleeves without ties, even without waistcoats, and shouted "bis" so frantically that Anna Vassilievna gave the order to row as quickly as possible to the other end of the lake. Before, however, the boat had time to moor at the bank, Uvar Ivanovich succeeded in surprising his friends for a second time: having noticed that in one spot the woods echoed every sound with peculiar clarity, he suddenly started to call like a quail. At first everyone was startled, but a moment later experienced genuine pleasure, for Uvar Ivanovich imitated the sound with remarkable skill. This encouraged him; he began to mew, but he wasn't quite so good at that; he gave one more imitation of the quail, looked round at everybody, and became silent. Shubin started to hug him, but he thrust him aside. At that moment the boat was tied up and they all climbed out on to the bank.

Meanwhile, the coachman, with the footman and the maid, had brought the baskets from the carriage and laid out luncheon on the grass under the old limes. Everybody sat round the out-spread table-cloth and started on the pâtés and other dishes. They all had good appetites, and Anna Vassilievna kept urging and encouraging her guests to eat more, maintaining that it was healthy to do so in the open air. She said this to Uvar Ivanovich, too. "Don't worry," he mumbled at her with his mouth full. "Hasn't God sent us a splendid day!" she kept on repeating. She was unrecognizable; she seemed to be twenty years younger. Bersenev remarked upon this. "Yes, yes," she said, "I was a fine figure of a girl in my day— you wouldn't have found me left out in the pick of any bunch."

Shubin kept close to Zoë and kept pouring out wine for her. She refused, he insisted, and ended by drinking the glass himself and offering her some more; he also announced to her that he wanted to rest his head in her lap— but she would not allow him to take such a "great liberty".

Elena seemed to be the most serious one of the party, yet she felt wonderfully calm inside, calmer than she had felt for a long time. She felt infinitely kind-hearted, too. She kept wanting to have Bersenev as well as Insarov sitting next to her. . . . Andrei Petrovich vaguely guessed at this and sighed in secret.

The hours flew by. Evening was drawing on. Anna Vassilievna suddenly became flustered. "Good heavens, how late it is!" she began; "we've eaten and drunk and it's time we wiped our lips." She began to fuss and everybody fussed with her; they got up and walked in the direction of the castle, where the carriages were waiting. As they passed the lakes, they all stopped to get a last view of Tsaritsin. The vivid colours of sunset flamed everywhere; the sky was red, the leaves, disturbed by a sudden breeze, glistened iridescently; the water in the distance flowed like liquid gold; the little red towers and summer-houses strewn here and there in the park stood out sharply against the dark green of the trees.

"Good-bye, Tsaritsin—we shall never forget this day!" murmured Anna Vassilievna.

But just then, and as if to confirm her last words, a curious incident occurred which was, indeed, not easy to forget. It happened like this. Hardly had Anna Vassilievna finished delivering her final farewell to Tsaritsin, when suddenly from behind a tall lilac-bush a few steps away there came a confused sound of laughter and shouting and exclamations, and a crowd of rough, dishevelled men— the same song-lovers who had so enthusiastically applauded Zoë—burst out on to the path. The song-lovers seemed to have had more than a drop too much. They stopped when they saw the ladies, but one of them, of huge stature, with a bull's neck and a bull's blood-shot eyes, detached himself from the others and, bowing clumsily and staggering

as he walked, came up to Anna Vassilievna, who was
petrified with fear.

"Bonne shoor, Madame," he mumbled in a hoarse
voice, "how do you do?"

Anna Vassilievna drew back.

"And why you," he went on in broken Russian, "not
wish sing bis when our Gesellschaft shout bis und bravo
und hoch. . . ."

"Yes, yes, why?" the Gesellschaft echoed.

Insarov wanted to step forward, but Shubin held him
back and stood shielding Anna Vassilievna.

"Permit me, esteemed stranger," he began, "to express the genuine amazement into which you plunge us all
by your behaviour. As far as I can see you belong to the
Saxon group of the Aryan race and we might therefore
have expected to find that you had some knowledge of
manners, whereas you have addressed yourself to a lady to
whom you have not been introduced. Believe me, at any
other time I, personally, would have been delighted to
make your acquaintance, because observing the remarkable development of your biceps, triceps and deltoid, I, as
a sculptor, would deem it the greatest happiness to engage
you as a model. But on this occasion, I beg you to leave
us."

The "esteemed" stranger listened to Shubin's speech,
screwing his head contemptuously to one side and with his
arms akimbo. "I not understand a word you say," he
mumbled at last. "You think I shoemaker? Or watch-
maker? Eh? I officer. Government service, yes!"

"I don't doubt it," Shubin was on the point of saying.

"Now *I* say," continued the stranger, pushing him
aside with a powerful arm, like a branch out of his path,

"I say why you not sing bis, when we shout bis? Now I go this minute but I will this Fräulein—not this dame, no, this I not will—but this one or this one (he pointed to Zoë and Elena) muss me give einen Kuss as we say in German, yes, a kiss. A Kuss, that is nothing."

"Nothing, einen Kuss," the Gesellschaft echoed again.

"Ah, der Sakramenter," mumbled one completely tipsy German, exploding with laughter.

Zoë seized Insarov by the hand, but he broke away from her and drew himself up in front of the huge ruffian.

"Will you please go immediately," he ordered in a low but firm voice.

The German laughed coarsely. "Go? I like that! I can walking where I like. Go? Why go?"

"Because you've dared to insult a lady," retorted Insarov, suddenly turning pale, "because you're drunk."

"What? I drunk? Hear you? Hören sie das, Herr Provisor? I Offizier and he dare. Now I demand die Satisfaktion. Einen Kuss will ich!"

"If you take another step . . ." began Insarov.

"Yes, what?"

"I'll throw you into the water."

"Into the water? Herr Je! Only that? Let us see, this is interesting, how you do it."

The Offizier lifted his arms and moved forward, but just then something unexpected occurred; he grunted, his huge body swayed, rose from the ground, his legs kicking in the air, and before the ladies had time to scream or anybody realized what was happening, the Offizier tumbled ponderously into the lake with a heavy splash and immediately disappeared under the whirling water.

"Ai!" the ladies shrieked in unison.

94

"Mein Gott!" exclaimed the others.

A minute passed, and a round head with wet hair plastered to the skull emerged from the water; the head in question was blowing bubbles, two hands were struggling convulsively at its lips.

"He's drowning, save him, he's drowning!" Anna Vassilievna shouted to Insarov, who stood on the bank, his legs apart, breathing heavily.

"He'll swim out all right," he murmured with contemptuous and merciless unconcern. "Let's go," he added, taking Anna Vassilievna by the arm, "let's go, Uvar Ivanovich, Elena Nikolaevna."

"———Ah———a— oh ah ———."

At that moment they heard the yells of the wretched German who had managed to get a grip on some rushes near the bank.

They all followed Insarov and had to pass in front of the Gesellschaft. But, having lost their leader, the rowdy creatures had quietened down and did not utter a word. Only one of their number, the bravest of the lot, muttered, shaking his head, "Donnerwetter, this is Gott weiss was . . . what more;" another one even raised his hat. Insarov struck them as very formidable and they were not mistaken: his face wore a dangerous and cruel expression. The Germans rushed to pull out their companion and the latter, as soon as he found himself on firm ground, began to swear tearfully and shout at the "Russian scoundrels", saying that he would lodge a complaint, go to his Excellency Count von Kieseritz himself. . . .

But the "Russian scoundrels" took no notice of his exclamations and hastened to the castle as quickly as they could. They were all silent as they walked through the park, only Anna Vassilievna muttered something now and then. But when they reached the carriages they stopped and broke into irresistible, irrepressible laughter, the laughter of Homeric heroes. The first to go off into crazy shrieks was Shubin, then came the pattering roll of Bersenev, then the thin tinkling pearls of Zoë; Anna Vassilievna, too, suddenly exploded, Elena could not help smiling, and even Insarov was unable to keep a straight face. But Uvar Ivanovich laughed louder, more heartily and longest of all. He laughed until his sides ached; he sneezed and gasped, was quiet for a moment and then mumbled through his tears, "I was just thinking . . . what was that splash . . .? And it was him—plop . . ." and at the last word, which he brought out convulsively, a new burst of laughter shook his whole frame. Zoë kept egging him on. "I could see," she said, "the legs kicking in the air." "Yes, yes," repeated Uvar Ivanovich, "the legs, and then splash—and there he was, plop. . . ."

"And how did he manage it?" Zoë asked. "The German was three times as big."

"I'll tell you how," answered Uvar Ivanovich, wiping his eyes, "I saw it. One hand round the waist, then he tripped him up, and then the splash—I heard it—and he went plop. . . ."

The carriages were well on their way, the Tsaritsin castle was long out of sight, before Uvar Ivanovich quietened down. Shubin, who again shared the phaeton with him, finally had to call him to order.

Insarov felt contrite. He sat in the carriage opposite Elena (Bersenev had seated himself on the box) and said nothing. She, too, did not utter a word. He thought she was criticizing his behaviour, but she wasn't criticizing him. She had been very frightened, at first, then she had been startled by the expression on his face, then she became thoughtful. She did not quite know what she was thoughtful about. The emotion she had experienced during the day had vanished—she was aware of that —but it had given place to another one, which as yet she did not quite understand. The *partie de plaisir* had lasted too long, the evening imperceptibly had turned into night. The carriage rolled on rapidly, now past ripening fields, where the air was close and fragrant and smelt of wheat, now past broad meadows whose sudden freshness hit one in the face like a light wave. The sky seemed to rise like smoke on the horizon. At last, red and dim, the moon came out. Anna Vassilievna dozed. Zoë peered out of the window, watching the road. Elena suddenly realized that more than an hour had passed since she had spoken to Insarov. She turned to him with an unimportant question. He answered her eagerly.

Strange sounds began to stir in the air—it was as if thousands of voices were talking in the distance. Moscow was rushing out to meet them. Lights began to twinkle in front of them and became more and more numerous. At last the cobbles rattled under their wheels. Anna Vassilievna woke up, everybody began to talk in the carriage, although nobody could hear what was being said—the cobbles rattled so loudly under the two carriages and the thirty-two hooves. The journey between Moscow and Kunzovo seemed long and dreary; they were all asleep or silent, their heads lolling towards their respective corners. Elena alone did not close her eyes; she could not tear them away from the dark silhouette of Insarov. Shubin was overcome with sadness. The breeze was blowing into

97

his eyes and this irritated him; he snuggled into the collar of his coat and was on the verge of crying. Uvar Ivanovich snored comfortably, rocking from side to side. At last the carriages stopped. Two footmen carried Anna Vassilievna out of the carriage—she was quite prostrate and, wishing good-night to her companions, declared that she was "half dead". They began thanking her, but she merely repeated, "half dead". Elena pressed Insarov's hand (for the first time) and remained sitting at her window for a long time without undressing. Shubin found time to whisper to Bersenev before he left, "Who else but a hero would go throwing drunken Germans into the water?"

"You didn't achieve anything like that," replied Bersenev, and went home with Insarov.

Dawn was already showing in the sky when the two friends reached their home. The sun had not yet risen, but the chill of daybreak was already making itself felt; a silvery dew had covered the grass and the first larks were trilling high, very high up in the misty depths of the sky, in which one last bright star glared down like a solitary eye.

# CHAPTER XVI

AFTER MEETING INSAROV, Elena started keeping a diary for the fifth or sixth time in her life. Here are some extracts from it:

*June.* . . . Andrei Petrovich brings me books but I can't read them. I'm ashamed of admitting it to him. I don't feel like lying to him, giving them back saying that I've read them. I believe it would upset him. He notices everything about me. He seems to be very much attached to me. He's a very good man, Andrei Petrovich.

. . . What is it I want? Why is my heart so heavy? So numb. Why do I watch the birds that fly past with such resentment? As though I'd like to fly away with them—I don't know where, but far, far away from here. Surely this is a sinful desire! My father, my mother, all my family are here. Is it that I don't love them? No, I don't love them in the way I'd like to. It makes me shudder to admit it, but it's the truth. Perhaps I'm a great sinner, perhaps that is why I feel so dejected, and restless. A strange hand seems to weigh on me and press me down. As if I were in a prison and the walls were on the verge of crumbling down on top of me. Why don't other people feel this? Whom, then, can I love if I feel nothing but coldness for my own family? Papa may be right when he says that I only love cats and dogs. I must think about this. I don't pray enough:

one should pray. . . . But I believe that I would know how to love. . . .

. . . I still feel shy with Mr. Insarov. I can't think why. I'm not a child, after all, and he's so simple and kind. Sometimes his face is very serious. Probably his thoughts are elsewhere. I realize this and feel guilty of taking up his time. Andrei Petrovich, that's a different matter. I could prattle with him the whole day long. But he, too, keeps talking to me about Insarov. And in what terrifying detail! I dreamt of him last night with a dagger in his hand. And he was saying to me, "I will kill you and kill myself." How silly!

. . . Oh, if only someone would say to me: This is what you should do. To be good is not enough. To do good —yes, that's the chief thing in life. But how does one set about it? Oh, if only I could learn to control myself. I can't understand why I go on thinking about Mr. Insarov. When he comes and sits beside me and listens attentively—but makes no effort himself, remains un-ruffled—I watch him and feel happy, and that's all. But when he goes I keep remembering his words and get annoyed with myself and even upset. . . . I don't know why. (He speaks bad French, but is not ashamed of it—I like that.) It is true that I always think a lot about new people. As I talked to him, I suddenly remembered our butler, Vassili, who dragged a crippled old man out of a burning hut at the risk of his own life. Papa called him a fine chap, Mamma gave him five roubles but I wanted to kneel down in front of him. He had a simple, even stupid, face, and later on became a drunkard.

. . . To-day I gave a kopeck to a beggar-woman and she asked me: Why do you look so sad? I'd no idea that I looked sad. I think it must be because I'm alone, always alone, with all my goodness, with all my wickedness. Nobody to stretch out a hand to. I don't want those who come to me, and those I would like to have near me go their own way. . . .

. . . I don't know what's the matter with me to-day, my head's in a whirl, I feel ready to fall down on my knees and beg and implore for mercy. I feel as if I were being tortured to death—why or by whom I have no idea—and inwardly protest and scream, and then I cry and can't stop the words coming out. Oh God, dear God, curb these outbreaks! You alone can do it—nothing else can, not my miserable almsgiving, nor study, nothing, nothing can help me. Sometimes I think I should go and work as a servant—really, it would be easier like that.

. . . What good is my youth, what am I alive for, why have I been given a soul—what's it all for?

. . . Insarov . . . Mr. Insarov—I really don't know what to call him—continues to occupy my thoughts. I would like to know what there is in his heart. He seems so open, so accessible, but not to my eyes. Sometimes he looks so searchingly at me—or is it only my imagination? Paul keeps teasing me—I'm cross with him. What does he want? He's in love with me, but I don't want his love. He's also in love with Zoë. I'm unjust towards him. He told me yesterday that I didn't know how to be unjust by halves. That is true. It is very wrong.

. . . Ah, I realise that a human being must go through misery, or poverty, or sickness, for it's so easy otherwise to become presumptuous.

. . . Why did Andrei Petrovich tell me to-day about those two Bulgarians? He seemed to do it with a purpose.

Mr. Insarov is no concern of mine. I'm angry with Andrei Petrovich.

. . . I'm taking up my pen . . . and I don't know where to start. How unexpectedly he spoke to me to-day in the garden. How tender and trustful he was. It all happened so quickly, as though we were old, very old friends, and had only just become aware of each other. How is it that I didn't understand him till now? And now how close he is to me. And this is what is so surprising—I've become so much calmer. How funny it is: yesterday I was angry with Andrei Petrovich, with him, too, I even called him Mr. Insarov, and to-day. . . . Here's a truthful man at last, a man one can rely on. He does not tell lies, he's the first man I've met who never lies. All the others do, everything is a lie. Andrei Petrovich, dear, kind Andrei Petrovich, why am I abusing you? No! Andrei Petrovich is possibly more learned than he is, maybe even more intelligent. But I don't know why he seems so small beside the other one. When the other one speaks of his country, he grows, he grows and becomes more handsome and his voice sounds like steel and you feel that he would not lower his eyes in front of anyone in the world. And it's not only talk—he has done things and will go on doing them. I will make him tell me all about it. . . . How he suddenly turned and smiled at me! . . . Only brothers smile in that way. Ah, how happy I am. When he first came to see us I never thought that we should become close friends so soon. Now I even feel a certain pleasure in the thought that I did not seem to care to begin with. . . . Did not seem to care? Do I care now?

. . . It's a long time since I have felt so calm inside. It is quiet, so quiet in my heart. There is nothing to write down. I see him often—that's all. What more is there to say?

. . . Paul has shut himself up. Andrei Petrovich seldom comes. I'm sorry, it seems to me that he. . . . No, it can't be that. I like talking to Andrei Petrovich, never about myself, always about something useful, purposeful. Not like with Shubin. Shubin is flashy like a butterfly, but he admires his own flashiness; butterflies don't do that. Anyway, both Shubin and Andrei Petrovich. . . . I know what I'd like to say. . . .

. . . He likes coming here, I know that. But why— what does he see in me? It is true that we have the same tastes. We don't like poetry, either of us, we don't know much about painting. But how much he is my superior. He is calm, and I'm eternally restless. He has a path to follow, an aim, whereas I, where am I going? Where is my nest? He is calm, but his thoughts are far away. The time will come when he will leave us for ever and go home over there, beyond the seas. Well, God be with him. All the same, I shall be happy to have known him while he was here. Why isn't he Russian? No, he couldn't be Russian. Mamma likes him too. "A modest man," is what she says about him. Dear, kind Mamma, she doesn't understand him. Paul is silent. He has just realized that I dislike his insinuations, but he is jealous of him. The wicked boy. What right has he got. . . .? Have I ever. . . . It's all so silly. Why do all these thoughts come crowding into my head?

. . . Isn't it strange, though, that up to now, and I'm twenty, I've never loved anybody? It seems to me that the reason why D. (I'll call him D., I like the name, Dmitri) has such serenity is that he has surrendered himself completely to his cause, to his dream. What has he got to worry about? A man who has surrendered himself completely, so completely, what more is there that he can do? He's not answerable any more. . . . It's not what *I* want, but what *it* wants. Incidentally, we both like the same flowers. I picked a rose to-day. A petal dropped off and he picked it up . . . I gave him the whole rose.

. . . D. often comes to see us. He spent the whole evening with us yesterday. He wants to teach me Bulgarian. I like being with him. I feel so at home with him. Better than at home.

. . . The days fly past. . . . I feel happy and—I don't know why  a little frightened and I want to give thanks to God and tears are not far away either. Oh, the warm, the balmy days. . . .

. . . Everything still seems light and easy to me—and only at times, only now and then, a little sadness creeps in. . . . I'm happy. Am I happy?

. . . I won't forget yesterday's trip for a long time. What strange, new, terrifying impressions! When he seized that giant and threw him into the water, like a ball, I wasn't frightened . . . but *he* frightened me. That sinister, almost cruel, face. And the way he said, "He'll swim out." My heart missed a beat. It means I didn't understand him. And then when everybody laughed, when I laughed, how it hurt, for his sake. He was ashamed, I knew it, he was ashamed because of me. He told me so later on in the carriage, in the dark, when I tried to make out his features and was afraid of him. No, no one can play the fool with him and he knows how to stand up for people. But why the rage, the trembling lips, the venom in the eyes? Maybe it can't be otherwise? A man can't be virile, a fighter, and remain gentle and meek? Life's a rough business, he said to me the other day. I repeated this to Andrei Petrovich—he did not agree with D. Which of them is right? And how beautifully that day began. How wonderful it was to walk at his side, even in silence. . . . But I'm glad that it all happened as it did. It had to happen.

. . . Restlessness again. . . . I don't feel well. . . .

. . . For days now I haven't written anything in this copy book. I didn't feel like it. I felt that whatever I might write, it wouldn't be what was really going on in my heart. . . . What is there in my heart? I had a long talk with him which opened my eyes to many things. He told me about his plans (by the way, I know now why he has a scar on his neck. . . . My God, when I think that he's been sentenced to death, that he escaped by the skin of his teeth, that he was wounded . . .). He expects war and is glad about it. But all the same I've never seen D. so sad. What can he . . . he! . . . be sad about? Papa returned from town, found us together and gave us a queer look. Andrei Petrovich came; I noticed that he has become very pale and thin. He reproached me for being far too cold and off-hand with Shubin. I'd forgotten the very existence of Paul. When I see him I'll try to make up for it. He doesn't matter to me at all any more . . . nor does anybody else in the whole world. Andrei Petrovich talked to me in a kind of compassionate way. What does it all mean? Why is everything so dark around me and within me? It seems that both without and within something mysterious is taking place . . . that I must find the right word for it.

. . . I didn't sleep during the night—my head aches. Why write? He went away too quickly to-day, just when

I so wanted to talk to him. He seems to be avoiding me. Yes, he is avoiding me!

. . . I have found the word, I have seen the light. Oh God, have pity on me. . . . I am in love!

# CHAPTER XVII

ON THE SAME day that Elena was writing this last, fateful word in her diary, Insarov sat in Bersenev's room, while Bersenev stood with a bewildered expression on his face. Insarov had just informed him of his decision to leave the next day for Moscow.

"But how ridiculous!" exclaimed Bersenev. "Why, it's the best part of the summer! What will you do in Moscow? Why this sudden decision? Have you had some news?"

"No, I haven't had any news," replied Insarov, "but in my opinion I oughtn't to stay here any longer."

"But how is it possible. . . ."

"Andrei Petrovich," murmured Insarov, "for mercy's sake, don't insist. I don't find it easy, either, to go away and leave you, but it has got to be done."

Bersenev looked at him fixedly. "I know that you can't be persuaded," he said at last. "So it's settled, is it?"

"Absolutely settled," said Insarov. He got up and walked out of the room.

Bersenev paced his room for a while, then took his hat and went to the Stakhovs.

"You've got something to tell me," Elena said to him as soon as they were left alone.

"Yes . . . how did you guess?"

"Never mind how. Tell me what it is."

Bersenev told her of Insarov's decision. Elena grew pale. "What can it mean?" she uttered with an effort.

"You know," murmured Bersenev, "that Dmitri Nikanorich doesn't like to account for his actions. But I believe that. . . . Let's sit down, Elena Nikolaevna, you don't look well. I believe I can guess the real reason for this sudden departure."

"What, what is the reason?" repeated Elena, pressing Bersenev's hand nervously between her own icy fingers, without noticing it.

"You see," Bersenev began with a sad smile,"—how can I explain this to you? I'll have to go back to last spring, to the time when I first began to know Insarov better. I'd met him at the house of a relation of mine, who had a very pretty daughter. It seemed to me that Insarov was attracted by her—and I asked him about it. He laughed and told me that I was mistaken, that his heart hadn't been touched, but that he would go away immediately if anything like that happened to him, because he didn't wish— these were his own words—to betray his cause and his duty for the satisfaction of a private emotion. 'I'm a Bulgarian,' he said, 'a Russian's love is no good to me'."

"Well . . . and now . . . what is it you . . ." whispered Elena, turning away her head like a person expecting a blow, but still keeping Bersenev's hand in hers.

"I believe," he murmured, also lowering his voice, "I believe that the thing that I had mistakenly suspected then has happened now."

"That is . . . you believe that. . . . Don't torture me!" Elena burst out.

"I believe," continued Bersenev hastily, "that Insarov

has fallen in love with a Russian girl and because of his vow
has decided to run away."

Elena squeezed his hand even more tightly and lowered
her head still more, as though trying to conceal from him
the guilty flush that had suddenly covered her face and
neck.

"Andrei Petrovich, you're kind, you're an angel," she
murmured, "but surely he'll come to say good-bye?"

"Yes, I'm sure he will. He wouldn't want to go away
without. . . ."

"Tell him, tell him that. . . ."

Here the poor girl could stand it no longer. Tears
streamed from her eyes and she ran out of the room.

"So that's how she loves him," thought Bersenev to
himself, slowly returning home. "I hadn't expected it, I
didn't think it had gone as deep as that. I'm kind, she
says," he continued meditatively. "Who knows on the
strength of what emotion and impulse I told all this to
Elena? Not out of kindness, certainly not out of kindness. . . . It's all this damnable longing to make sure that
the dagger is really in the wound. . . . I ought to be glad
—they love one another and I have been an instrument to
that end. . . . 'The future intermediary between Science
and the Russian public,' Shubin calls me. Evidently it's my
destiny to be an intermediary. But supposing I'm mistaken? No, I can't be mistaken. . . ."

Andrei Petrovich felt a great bitterness in his heart and
his mind refused to take in Raumer.

The next day, about two in the afternoon, Insarov came
to the Stakhovs'. As if on purpose, a visitor was sitting at
that moment in Anna Vassilievna's drawing-room—a
neighbour, the archpriest's wife, a worthy, admirable

woman, who had had some trouble with the police because she had suddenly taken it into her head at the height of a very hot day, to bathe in a pond adjoining a main road, often frequented by an important official's family. The presence of a stranger was at first a relief to Elena, from whose face the blood had ebbed as soon as she heard Insarov's step, but her heart sank at the thought that he might say good-bye without having had a word with her alone. He seemed embarrassed and avoided her eyes. "Is he really going to say good-bye now?" she thought. Insarov, in fact, was turning towards Anna Vassilievna. Elena got up quickly and called him aside to the window. The archpriest's wife tried to turn round in surprise, but she wore such tight corsets that they squeaked whenever she moved. She stayed where she was.

"Listen to me," Elena murmured hurriedly, "I know why you've come to-day. Andrei Petrovich has told me about your decision, but I beg you, I implore you, not to say good-bye to us to-day, but to come early to-morrow, about eleven. I must have a few words with you."

Insarov bowed his head in silence.

"I won't keep you now. . . . You promise?"

Insarov bowed his head again, but said nothing.

"Lenochka, come here," murmured Anna Vassilievna. "Look what a lovely reticule Matushka* has."

"I embroidered it myself," remarked the priest's wife.

Elena walked away from the window.

Insarov did not stay more than a quarter of an hour at the Stakhovs'. Elena watched him stealthily. He fidgeted about, continued to avoid looking anybody in the face and

* Matushka: a derivative of Mother, used in addressing priests' wives.—*Translator's note.*

went away in an odd, abrupt manner—just disappeared.

The day dragged on slowly for Elena; the long, long night seemed even more interminable. Elena either sat on her bed, with her arms clutching her knees, and her head resting against them, or walked up to the window and pressed her burning forehead to the cold window-pane, and thought and thought, driving herself with always the same thoughts into a state of exhaustion. Her heart seemed either to have turned to stone or to have taken leave of her body—she did not feel it any more, although the blood throbbed heavily in her head and her hair seemed to burn her and her lips were dry. "He'll come, he hasn't said good-bye to Mamma . . . he won't fail me. . . . Did Andrei Petrovich really tell the truth? It isn't possible. He didn't promise in so many words. . . . Have I really parted from him for ever?" Such were the thoughts that never left her, that were with her continuously . . . neither coming nor going but, like a mist, fluctuating perpetually inside her head. "He loves me"—the thought suddenly ran like a flame through her whole being and she stared into the darkness; a secret smile, no one could see, parted her lips . . . but she instantly shook her head, clasped her hands behind her neck and once again the familiar thoughts swam like a mist in her head. She undressed just before dawn and got into bed, but could not sleep. The morning sun's fierce rays broke into her room. "Oh, but if he really loves me!" she suddenly exclaimed, and unashamed of the light that suddenly enveloped her, she opened her arms to it.

She got up, dressed herself, and went downstairs. Everybody else was still asleep in the house. She went into the garden, but it was so calm and green there, so fresh;

and the birds chirruped so trustfully, the flowers looked so gay, that she felt afraid. "Oh," she thought, "if it is true, there's not a blade of grass happier than I am—but *is* it true?" She went back to her room and to kill time began to change her dress. But everything fell from her hands, slipped out of them, and she was still sitting half-dressed in front of her dressing-table when she was called to tea. She went down. Her mother noticed that she was pale, but merely said, "How nice you're looking to-day." And, throwing a cursory glance at her, added, "That frock suits you, you should always wear it when you want to look your best."

Elena did not answer and sat down in a corner.

Nine o'clock struck—two more hours before eleven. Elena picked up a book, then her sewing, then the book again; then she pledged herself to walk up and down the path a hundred times and did so; then for a long time she watched Anna Vassilievna playing patience . . . when she looked at the time, it wasn't yet ten. Shubin came into the drawing-room. She tried to talk to him and apologized to him, she didn't know why. . . . It wasn't that speaking was an effort, but every word seemed to be meaningless. Shubin bent towards her . . . She was expecting him to laugh at her, but on raising her eyes she found herself looking into a sad and friendly face. She smiled at him. Shubin also smiled in silence and softly walked out of the room. She wanted to make him stay, but forgot for a moment what to call him. At last the clock struck eleven. She began to wait, wait, wait and listen. There was nothing left that she could do. She had even stopped thinking. Her heart seemed to come back to life and began to thump louder and louder, and strangely enough, time seemed to rush by more quickly. A quarter of an hour passed, half an hour, then a few minutes, so she thought, and suddenly she started—the clock struck, not twelve, but one o'clock.

"He won't come, he'll go away without saying good-bye." The thought welled into her head on a fresh surge of blood. She gasped for breath; she was on the verge of tears. She rushed to her room and tumbled across her bed, her face buried on her clasped hands. She lay motionless for half an hour. Tears fell on the pillow, trickling through her fingers. Then, all at once, she raised herself and sat up; something unusual was going on inside her; her face changed, her tear-stained eyes suddenly dried of themselves and sparkled, her brows were drawn, her lips pressed together. Another half hour went by. For the last time Elena pricked up her ears to see if she could hear the familiar voice, then she got up, put on a hat, some gloves, threw a cape over her shoulders and, slipping unseen out of the house, walked briskly along the road that led to Bersenev's lodgings.

# CHAPTER XVIII

ELENA WALKED ON, her head bent, her eyes set in a
fixed stare. She was afraid of nothing, she was aware of
nothing. All she wanted was to see Insarov once more.
She walked on, not realizing that the sun had disappeared
long ago behind heavy black clouds, that the wind was
whistling fiercely among the trees and blowing her dress
about, that the dust rose suddenly and raced in clouds
along the road. Large drops of rain began to fall, but she
did not notice them either. The rain began to fall faster
and harder, and was followed by lightning and thunder.
Elena stopped and looked around. Fortunately, not far
from where the storm had overtaken her, there was a
small chapel, ancient and deserted, built over a derelict
well. She ran towards it and found shelter under its low
roof. The rain was now falling in torrents and the sky was
completely overcast. In silent despair, Elena stared at the
dense network of swiftly falling rain drops. The last hope
of seeing Insarov had gone. An old beggar-woman walked
into the chapel, shook herself, murmured as she bowed
deeply, "Out of the rain, lady," and groaning and grunt-
ing sat down on the step by the well. Elena put her hand in
her pocket. The old woman noticed the movement and
her face, wrinkled and yellow, but with signs of former
beauty, brightened up.

"Thank you, dear benefactress," she began. Despite

the fact that Elena had no purse in her pocket, the old woman was already stretching out her hand.

"I have no money, my good woman," said Elena, "but here, take this, it might come in useful." She gave her her handkerchief.

"Oh, my beauty," muttered the beggar, "what will I do with this kerchief? Maybe give it to my grand-daughter when she goes to get married? May God bless you for your kindness."

There was a peal of thunder. "The Lord Jesus Christ," she muttered, and made the sign of the cross three times. "I believe I've seen you before," she added after a pause. "Didn't you cross my palm the other day?"

Elena looked at the old woman and recognized her. "Yes, I did," she replied, "And you asked me why I looked so sad?"

"So you were, dearie, so you were. I knew I'd seen you before. And you look sad and troubled now. Your handkerchief is all wet from crying. Oh, you poor young dears, it's always the same trouble with you, the same heavy sorrow!"

"What sorrow, grannie?"

"What sorrow? Ah, dear young lady, it's no use trying to deceive an old woman like me. I know what your trouble is; and you are not the only one either. I was young, too, once upon a time, and had the same heartache. Yes. But I'll tell you this, in return for your kindness: you've got a good man there, not a flighty one. Hold fast to him, cling to him like grim death. If it has to be, it will be, if not, it's God's own will. Yes. What are you looking at me like that for? I can tell you what the future holds all right. Want me to take all your sorrows away with this handkerchief? I will, and it'll be the end of it. See, the rain's become just a drizzle. You wait here a bit and I'll go. I've been out in the wet before. So remember, dearie, the sorrow's come, the sorrow's gone, and there's no trace of it left. God bless you!"

The beggar-woman got up from the edge of the well, went out of the chapel and on her way. Elena looked after her with amazement. "What does it mean?" she could not help murmuring.

The rain became thinner and thinner, the sun shone for a moment. Elena was on the point of leaving her shelter. Suddenly, about ten yards away from the chapel, she saw Insarov. Wrapped in a cloak, he was walking along the same road which Elena had just taken. He seemed to be hurrying home.

She leaned against the old rail of the porch; she wanted to call him, but her voice failed her. Insarov was already hurrying past without looking up. . . .

"Dmitri Nikanorich!" she managed to say at last.

Insarov stopped short, looked round. At first he did not recognize Elena, but came up to her at once.

"You! You here?" he exclaimed. She stepped back into the chapel without a word. He followed her. "You here?" he repeated.

She still said nothing and just gazed at him steadily and tenderly. He lowered his eyes.

"Were you coming from our house?"

"No . . . not from your house."

"No?" Elena repeated, and tried to smile. "Is that how you keep your promises? I've been waiting for you since this morning."

"I didn't promise anything yesterday, Elena Nikolaevna, if you remember."

Elena again smiled faintly and ran her hand over her face. Both her hand and face were very pale.

"So you wanted to leave without saying good-bye to us?"

"Yes," Insarov replied in a stern, dull voice.

"What! After our friendship, our talks, after everything. . . . So that if I hadn't met you here by chance . . . (Elena's voice rang out sharply and she paused for a moment) . . . you would have gone and not held my hand for the last time . . . and not felt sorry?"

Insarov turned away. "Elena Nikolaevna, please, don't talk like that, I feel miserable enough as it is. Believe me, my decision has been taken at the cost of a great effort. If only you knew. . . ."

"I don't want to know," Elena interrupted apprehensively, "—why are you going. . . . It seems it must be so. It seems we have to part. You wouldn't want to hurt your friends without a good reason. But do friends part like this? For we *are* friends, aren't we?"

"No," said Insarov.

"What?" murmured Elena. A slight flush coloured her cheeks.

"That's precisely why I'm going, because we're not friends. Don't force me to say what I don't want to say, what I won't say."

"You've always been frank with me before," Elena said a shade reproachfully, "Do you remember?"

"Then I could afford to be frank, I had nothing to conceal, but now. . . ."

"But now?" asked Elena.

"But now . . . now I must go away. Good-bye. . . ."

Had Insarov raised his eyes to look at Elena at that

117

moment, he would have seen that her face became lighter and lighter as his grew darker and the frown deepened on his brow, but he was staring fixedly at the ground.

"Well, good-bye, Dmitri Nikanorich," she began; "but as we have met now, at least give me your hand in parting."

Insarov was on the point of holding out his hand. "No, I can't even do that," he muttered, and turned away again.

"You can't?"

"I can't. Good-bye." And he turned to the door of the chapel.

"Wait another moment," said Elena. "You seem to be afraid of me. But I'm braver than you are," she added, feeling herself shiver slightly all over. "I can tell you . . . do you want me to tell you? . . . why you found me here? Do you know where I was going?"

Insarov looked at her in surprise.

"I was coming to you."

"To me?"

Elena covered her face with her hands. "You wanted to make me say that I love you," she whispered. "Well, I've said it."

"Elena!" cried Insarov.

She took her hands away, looked at him, and fell on his breast. He held her in his arms—and remained silent. He did not need to tell her that he loved her. By the tone of his exclamation, by the sudden transformation of his whole being, by the rise and fall of his breast which she clung to so confidently, by the way he touched her hair with his fingers, Elena could not but feel that he loved her. He was silent—and she had no need of words. "He is here, he loves me . . . what more can I want?" The stillness of rapture, the stillness of an unyielding anchor, of an end accomplished; the supreme stillness that gives beauty and meaning even to death, endued her with its divine potency. She wanted nothing because she had everything.

"Oh, my brother, my friend, my love!" her lips whispered, and she could not tell if it was her heart or his that throbbed so blissfully and meltingly in her breast.

He stood motionless; his strong arms held in a close embrace the young life that had surrendered itself to him; and he felt against his breast a new and infinitely precious burden. A feeling of beatitude, of ineffable thankfulness, shook the strong roots of his heart, and for the first time in his life tears welled up in his eyes.

But she, she did not cry; she only repeated, "Oh, my friend, my brother."

"So you'll come with me wherever I go?" he asked her a quarter of an hour later, still holding her and supporting her in his arms.

"Wherever you go—to the end of the world. Where you are, I'll be there too."

"And you aren't deluding yourself? You know that your parents will never agree to our marriage?"

"I'm not deluding myself, I know it."

"You know that I'm poor, almost a beggar?"

"I do."

"That I'm not Russian, that it isn't my destiny to live in Russia, that you'll have to sever all your ties with your country, your people?"

"I do, I do."

"You know, too, that I've dedicated myself to a hard, unrewarding task, that I, that we, may have to face not only dangers but poverty and humiliation?"

E                                      119

"Yes, I know it all . . . I love you."

"That you will have to give up all the things you are used to, that alone out there among strangers you may have to work. . . .?"

She put her hand over his mouth. "I love you, my dearest one."

He began to kiss the slender, rosy fingers passionately. Elena did not pull away her hand from his lips and, with childish delight, and laughing curiosity, watched him cover her hand and her fingers with his kisses. Suddenly she flushed and hid her face against his breast. He raised her head tenderly and looked deeply into her eyes

"Welcome then," he said to her, "my wife before man and before God!"

## CHAPTER XIX

AN HOUR LATER Elena, a hat in one hand, a cape in the other, walked quietly into the drawing room of the villa. Her hair was slightly dishevelled and there was a small pink patch on each cheek; her lips refused to stop smiling and her eyes, which seemed ready to close and were indeed half-closed, went on smiling too. She could hardly walk from weariness, but it was a pleasant kind of weariness—in fact, everything seemed pleasant to her. Everything seemed friendly and gentle. Uvar Ivanovich sat by the window; she went up to him, put her hand on his shoulder, stretched herself a little and could not help laughing.

"What is it?" he asked in surprise.

She didn't know what to say. She wanted to kiss him. "Plop . . . !" she murmured at last. But Uvar Ivanovich did not move an eye-lid and went on looking at Elena with surprise. She dropped her cape and hat in his lap.

"Dear Uvar Ivanovich," she said, "I want to sleep, I'm worn out." And again she laughed and dropped into a chair beside him.

"Hm . . ." grunted Uvar Ivanovich, and twiddled his fingers. "You should . . . yes. . . ."

Elena looked around and thought—I'll soon have to part with all this. How strange! I'm not afraid, I have no doubts, no regrets. . . . No, I'm sorry about Mamma.

Then again she saw the chapel in her mind's eye; she heard his voice; she felt his arms around her. Her heart stirred happily, though faintly,—the exhaustion of happiness weighed upon it, too. She remembered the beggar-woman. "Yes, she did take away my sorrow," she thought. "How happy I am, and with what a sudden undeserved happiness." If she had given way even a little then, fond tears would have streamed unhindered from her eyes. She only kept them back by laughing all the time. Whatever position she adopted seemed to her the best one—she felt as if she were being rocked in a cradle. All her movements were graceful and deliberate. What had happened to her clumsiness and flurry?

Zoë appeared and Elena thought she had never seen a more charming little face. Anna Vassilievna walked in— there was a pang in Elena's heart, but with what tenderness she put an arm round her dear mamma and kissed her forehead where it met her slightly greying hair. Then she went to her room. How everything welcomed her there! With what mixed feelings of victory and humility she sat down on her bed, on the same bed where three hours before she had gone through such bitter moments! "But I already knew then that he loved me," she thought, "and even before. . . . Ah, no, no, that's a wicked thought." "You are my wife . . ." she whispered, burying her head in her hands and sinking down on her knees.

Towards evening she became more thoughtful. It was sad to think that she wouldn't see Insarov for some time. He could not remain at Bersenev's without arousing suspicion and that is why they had come to the following decision: Insarov was to return to Moscow and come to see them a few times before the autumn. In her turn, she promised to write and, if possible, arrange to meet him somewhere near by, near Kunzovo.

She came down to tea and found the whole family there and Shubin, who looked at her quizzically as soon as she appeared. Her first impulse was to greet him in her old friendly way, but she was afraid of his powers of observation, afraid of herself. She realized that it wasn't for nothing that he had left her in peace for the past fortnight.

Before long Bersenev arrived and brought Anna Vassilievna a message from Insarov, apologizing for his having left for Moscow without paying his respects. Insarov's name was mentioned for the first time that day in front of Elena; she felt her cheeks growing hot. She knew, moreover, that she ought to express regret at the sudden departure of a good friend, but she could not make herself pretend, and so stayed still and said nothing, while Anna Vassilievna exclaimed and made out how sorry she was. Elena tried to keep close to Bersenev for, although he knew a certain amount about her secret, she felt that under his wing she was safer from Shubin, who kept watching her, not teasingly, but intently. Throughout the evening, Bersenev could not help feeling surprised, he had expected to find Elena sadder than she was. Luckily for her, Shubin and he began talking about art; they moved away and she heard their voices as in a dream. Gradually, not only they, but the whole room, everything around her, began to appear to her as in a dream—everything: the samovar on the table and Uvar Ivanovich's short waistcoat and Zoë's polished nails and the oil painting of the Grand Duke Constantin Pavlovich on the wall—everything withdrew into the background, became enveloped in a haze and ceased to exist. She was only sorry for them all. "Why do they go on living?" she thought.

"Are you feeling sleepy, Lenochka?" her mother asked her. She did not hear her mother's question.

"An insinuation that's half-true, you say. . . . ?" These words, sharply uttered by Shubin, suddenly roused Elena's attention. "But surely," he went on, "that's the whole value of the thing. An insinuation that's true only makes you feel miserable—it's uncharitable; you remain indifferent to an insinuation that's false—it's merely silly; but one that's half-true is irritating and makes one impatient. For instance, if I say that Elena Nikolaevna is in love with one of us, what kind of insinuation would that be, eh?"

"Ah, M'sieu Paul," murmured Elena, "I'd like to show you that I'm annoyed, but I simply can't. I'm too tired."

"Why don't you go and lie down then?" muttered Anna Vassilievna, who always dozed in the evenings and was therefore eager to pack other people off to bed. "Say good-night and God speed you to bed. Andrei Petrovich will excuse you."

Elena kissed her mother, said good-night to the others, and left them. Shubin accompanied her to the door.

"Elena Nikolaevna," he whispered to her on the threshold, "you trample on M'sieu Paul, you use him mercilessly as a door mat, but M'sieu Paul worships you —your feet, the shoes on your feet and the soles of your shoes."

Elena shrugged her shoulders, reluctantly stretched out her hand—not the one that Insarov had kissed—and on reaching her room undressed at once, got into bed and went to sleep. She fell into a deep untroubled sleep—even children do not sleep like that, only a child recovering from an illness, with its mother sitting by its bedside, watching it and listening to its breathing.

## CHAPTER XX

"COME INTO MY room for a moment," Shubin said to Bersenev as soon as the latter had said good-bye to Anna Vassilievna. "I have something to show you."

Bersenev went with him to his part of the house. He was astonished by the number of statuettes, busts, studies, draped in wet cloths, standing about the room.

"I see you're working quite seriously," he remarked to Shubin.

"One's got to do something," the latter replied, "if one thing fails you, you've got to try another. Though, like a true Corsican, I'm busier with vendettas than with pure art. *Trema, Bisanzia!*"

"I don't catch your meaning," muttered Bersenev.

"Wait and see. Please have a look, my good friend and patron, at my Vendetta No. 1." Shubin unwrapped one of the figures and Bersenev saw a remarkable, very life-like bust of Insarov. Shubin had caught a likeness in the smallest of details and the expression he had given them was most impressive—honest, noble, daring. Bersenev was delighted.

"But this is wonderful!" he exclaimed. "My congratulations! It ought to be exhibited at once. Why do you call this splendid work a vendetta?"

"Because, my dear sir, I intend to present what you are pleased to call this splendid work to Elena Nikolaevna on our artists are so generously endowed. You've libelled yourself."

"You think so?" Shubin murmured tragically. "If there's no sign yet and if such a sign does appear, it'll be the fault of . . . a certain person. D'you know," he added, frowning in a sinister way, "that I've already taken to drink?"

"Liar."

"I swear to you I have," replied Shubin, and suddenly his face lit up with a smile. "But I didn't care for it, my boy, it doesn't go down my throat and my head feels like a drum afterwards. The great Lushchikin himself, Kharlampi Lushchikin, the greatest nozzler in Moscow—some say the greatest in all Russia—declared that I lacked promise. He says I've no feeling for the bottle."

Bersenev made as if to smash the group, but Shubin stopped him.

"No, my friend, don't smash it, it will serve as an object lesson, as a scarecrow."

Bersenev laughed. "In that case I'm ready to spare your scarecrow," he uttered, "and long live pure art for ever and ever!"

"Long may it live!" added Shubin. "With Art, good becomes more good and evil not so bad!"

The two friends shook each other firmly by the hand and went their different ways.

# CHAPTER XXI

ELENA'S FIRST REACTION on waking up was to feel frightened by her happiness. "Is it possible, is it really possible?" she kept asking herself and her heart faltered. Memories came flooding into her mind and she allowed herself to be overwhelmed by them. Then again a sublime, ecstatic peace enveloped her. In the course of the morning however she was oppressed by a certain anxiety, and the following days found her sad and despondent. It is true that she knew now what she wanted, but this did not make things any easier. That unforgettable encounter had lifted her irrevocably out of her old groove; she had left it for ever, she was far away, while everything around her went on as usual, went on in the same old way, as though nothing had changed. The old life continued as before and depended as before on her help and participation. She tried to start writing to Insarov, but that, too, did not work. On paper her words seemed lifeless or insincere. She had finished with her diary—drawn a long line under the last entry. That belonged to the past. All her thoughts, her whole being, belonged now to the future. She felt miserable. It seemed to her almost criminal to sit with her unsuspecting mother, to listen to her, to answer her questions, to talk to her. She felt all the time that she was leading a double life, was angry with herself, although she had no cause to feel ashamed. She was often overcome by an almost irresistible desire to confess everything, to hold nothing back, regardless of the consequences. "Why," she wondered, "didn't Dmitri take me away with him wherever he wanted to go, then and there, from the chapel? Didn't he say that I was his wife before God? Why am I here?" She began to fight shy of everybody, even Uvar Ivanovich, who became more and more bewildered and twiddled his fingers more than ever. Her very environment had become unsympathetic and cold. It was no longer like a dream, but rather a nightmare, a steady, deathly pressure on her heart, reproaching her and criticizing her and wanting to have nothing more to do with her. You belong to us, whatever you may think, it seemed to say. . . . Even her nestlings, her helpless birds and animals watched her—or so she imagined—with mistrust and hostility. She was ashamed of her feelings, humiliated by them. "It's my home, after all," she thought, "my family, my country. . . ." "No," another voice whispered to her, "not your country any more, nor your family. . . ." She was overcome with fear and was angry with herself for her lack of courage. The ordeal had only just begun and she was already losing patience. Was that what she had promised him? It took her some time, nevertheless, to regain control of herself.

A week passed, then another. Elena became calmer and more accustomed to her new attitude to life. She wrote two little notes to Insarov and took them to the post herself—she could never have confided in a maid, partly from shyness, partly from pride. She began to wait for Insarov to come in person. But, one fine day, instead of him, Nikolai Artemievich turned up.

# CHAPTER XXII

NOBODY IN HIS house had ever seen Stakhov, retired Captain of the Guards, so sour and at the same time so self-assured and pompous as he was that day. He walked into the drawing-room in his hat and coat. Stepping slowly, with his legs wide apart and clacking his heels, he advanced towards the looking-glass and studied his face for a long time, shaking his head calmly but severely, and biting his lips. Anna Vassilievna greeted him with outward anxiety but inward delight (she never felt anything else in his presence). He did not even remove his hat, said nothing to her and in silence let Elena kiss his leather glove. Anna Vassilievna started questioning him about his cure—he did not reply, Uvar Ivanovich came in, he glanced at him and said, "Bah!" He treated Uvar Ivanovich for the most part In a cold and patronizing way, though he admitted that there were "some traces of genuine Stakhov blood" in him. It is well known that almost every aristocratic family in Russia is convinced of the existence of exceptional hereditary traits peculiar to itself alone. We have often heard discussions "between ourselves" about the Perepreev neck and the Podsalaskin nose.

Zoë came in and curtsied to Nikolai Artemievich. He grunted and sank down into a chair, demanded some coffee, and only then took off his hat. Coffee was brought to him, he drank a cup, and having looked at everybody in turn, muttered through his teeth, "Sortez, s'il vous plaît," and, turning to his wife, added, "Et vous, madame, restez, je vous prie."

Everybody left the room except Anna Vassilievna. Her very head was wobbling with excitement. The pompousness of Nikolai Artemievich's behaviour disconcerted her. She was expecting something very unusual.

"What's the matter?" she exclaimed as soon as the door had closed.

Nikolai Artemievich threw her a casual glance.

"Nothing's the matter. What a way you always have of looking martyred," he began, dropping the corners of his mouth quite unnecessarily at every word. "I only wanted to warn you that we're having a new guest to dinner to-night."

"Who is it?"

"Kurnatovski, Egor Andreevich. You don't know him. He's the Chief Secretary of the Senate."

"He's going to dine with us to-night?"

"Yes."

"And in order to tell me that you had to ask everybody to leave the room?"

Nikolai Artemievich threw another glance at Anna Vassilievna, this time an ironical one.

"You're surprised? Well, don't be surprised too soon."

He was silent. Anna Vassilievna also remained silent for a time. "I would like . . ." she began.

Nikolai Artemievich suddenly interrupted her. "I know that you've always considered me an immoral person. . . ."

"I?" murmured Anna Vassilievna in astonishment.

". . . And you may be right. I don't wish to deny that I have in fact sometimes given you legitimate cause for grievance . . . (the grey roans! thought Anna Vassilievna in a flash) . . . although you yourself must admit that in a certain respect your health. . . .''

"But I'm not blaming you at all, Nikolai Artemievich."

"C'est possible. In any case, I have no intention of finding excuses for myself. Time will prove me right. But I consider it my duty to assure you that I am aware of my responsibilities and can see my way to meeting . . . to meeting my obligations as far as my family is concerned."

What does it all mean? Anna Vassilievna asked herself. (She could not know that the day before, in the English Club, in the corner of the lounge, an argument had arisen about the inability of Russians to make speeches. "Can any of us make a speech? Can you name even one?" one of the members had asked. "Well, what about Stakhov, for instance?" another had retorted, pointing at Nikolai Artemievich, who was standing near, and who almost whooped with delight.)

"For instance, my daughter Elena," continued Nikolai Artemievich; "don't you consider that it is time she took a definite step along the path . . . what I mean to say is, got married. All these intellectual capers, all this philanthropy is all very well, but within certain limits, up to a certain age. It is time for her to come down out of the clouds, to give up the society of all these artists, scholars and Montenegrins and become like everybody else.

"What meaning am I to ascribe to your words?" asked Anna Vassilievna.

"Well, pray listen to the end," replied Nikolai Artemievich with the same dropping of the lips. "I must tell you quite frankly, without evasion, that I made the acquaintance of this young man, Mr. Kurnatovski—I approached him—in the hope of having him as my son-in-law. I venture to believe that when you see him you will not accuse me of partiality or impulsiveness. (Nikolai Artemievich went on speaking, admiring his own eloquence.) His upbringing is all that can be desired; he was educated in the Law School; has perfect manners; is thirty-three years of age; is Chief Secretary with the rank of counsellor and has the collar of the Order of St. Stanislas. I hope you will do me the justice to admit that I'm not one of those *pères de comédie* who dream of nothing but rank. You yourself have told me, indeed, that Elena Nikolaevna likes steady, self-confident types. Egor Andreevich has a great head for business. On the other hand, my daughter has a weakness for deeds of generosity. Well, you ought to know then that Egor Andreevich, as soon as he reached the stage—you understand me—reached the stage when he could live respectably on his salary, immediately relinquished the annual allowance his father made him in favour of his brothers."

"Who is his father?" asked Anna Vassilievna.

"His father? He is also well-known in his way, a man of high principles, *un vrai stoicien*, a retired major, I believe, estate-bailiff to the Counts B . . . ."

"Oh?" murmured Anna Vassilievna.

"Oh? Why oh?" asked Nikolai Artemievich. "Are you, too, eaten up with prejudices?"

"But I didn't say anything," began Anna Vassilievna.

"Of course you did, you said 'Oh!' . . . Well, be that as it may, I thought it necessary to let you know what was in my mind and I venture to believe, to hope indeed, that Mr. Kurnatovski will be received *à bras ouverts*. He isn't a species of Montenegrin."

"Naturally, only I must send for Vanka the cook and order another course."

"You know that's not my department," muttered Nikolai Artemievich. He got up, put on his hat and, whistling away (somebody had told him that whistling except in one's summer villa or in a riding-school simply isn't done) went for a stroll in the garden. Shubin glanced at him from his window and put out his tongue at him in silence.

At ten minutes to four a hired carriage rolled up to the porch of the Stakhovs' villa and a man, still young, of prepossessing appearance and dressed with elegant simplicity, got out of it and gave his name to the footman. It was Egor Andreevich Kurnatovski.

This, among other things, is what Elena wrote to Insarov the next day.

"You may congratulate me, dear Dmitri, I have a suitor. He dined with us yesterday. Papa met him, I believe, at the English Club and asked him to dinner. He didn't come last night as a suitor, of course, but my kind Mamma, to whom Papa had confided his hopes, whispered to me who the guest was. His name is Egor Andreevich Kurnatovski. He is Chief Secretary of the Senate. I will describe his appearance to you first. He is not tall, smaller than you are, well built, with regular features, his hair is cut short and he wears long side-whiskers. He has small eyes (like yours), brown, alert; flat, wide lips; there is a perpetual smile in his eyes and on his lips, an official smile, as though it were on duty there. He has an easy manner, speaks very correctly—everything about him is correct; he eats, laughs, walks, all as if he were doing something important. 'How much she knows about him, you may be thinking at this minute. Yes, so that I can describe him to you. And how, pray, should one not learn a lot about one's suitor! There's something steely in him, and limited and futile at the same time, and honest, too; they say he is, indeed, very honest. You, my dear, are also made of steel, but in a different way from him. He sat next to me at table, Shubin opposite. At first the conversation was about some commercial enterprises—they say he knows something about them and almost gave up his job to run a large manufacturing concern. A pity he didn't do so. Then Shubin started talking about the theatre. Mr. Kurnatovski declared—and, I must admit, without any false modesty—that he knew nothing about art. It reminded me of you, but I thought to myself: no, all the same, Dmitri and I are ignorant in another way about art. What he seemed to want to say was: I don't understand it and it's not a necessity, of course, but there's a place for it in a well-organized state. He doesn't seem to be much interested in Petersburg society and the *comme il faut*, and even once called himself a proletarian. We, the workers, he said! I thought to myself: if Dmitri had said that, I shouldn't have liked it; but he—well, let him speak, let him boast! He was very polite with me, but it seemed to me all the time that I was talking to an exceedingly condescending head of a department. When he wants to praise someone he says that he has 'standards'—that's his favourite expression. He must be very assiduous, self-assured, capable of sacrifice (you see I'm impartial), that is, of sacrificing his own interest, but he's a bully. It would be fatal to fall into his hands. At table, somebody raised the question of bribes.

" 'I'm well aware,' he said, 'that in many cases the man

who accepts bribes is not guilty—he couldn't behave otherwise—but if he's found out there is nothing to do but sacrifice him.'

" 'Sacrifice an innocent man?' I cried.

" 'Yes, because of the principle.'

" 'What principle?' asked Shubin.

"Kurnatovski, somewhat embarrassed or surprised, said, 'There is surely no need to explain that.'

"Papa, who seems to worship him, hastened to say, too, that of course there was no need, and to my annoyance, the subject was dropped. In the evening, Bersenev came and began a terrible argument with him. I'd never before seen our kind Andrei Petrovich so excited. Mr. Kurnatovski did not for a moment deny the importance of science, of universities etc. . . . but I could well understand Andrei Petrovich's indignation. In his opinion they're all a form of drill. Shubin came up to me after dinner and said: this man here and the other one (he can't bring himself to utter your name) are both practical people, but look, what a difference! With the other one it's a true, a genuine ideal, held out by life itself—while here it's not even a sense of duty, merely official honesty and efficiency without any significance.

"Shubin is clever and I remembered these words for you. As for myself, I don't see what there is in common between you two. You have faith, which the other one hasn't got, because faith in oneself alone is not enough.

"He went away late, but Mamma had time to whisper to me that I had met with his approval and that Papa was delighted. Maybe he said about me, too, that I had standards? I almost told Mamma that I was very sorry, but that

I already had a husband. . . . Why does Papa hate you so! With Mamma it would have been possible to . . .

"Oh, my dearest! I described this gentleman to you in such detail in order to deaden my longing. I don't exist without you. I keep seeing, hearing you. . . . I'll be waiting for you, but not here, as you originally wanted—you can well imagine how difficult and awkward it would be for us! But, as I wrote to you, you remember, in that little wood . . . . My dearest, how I love you."

# CHAPTER XXIII

ABOUT THREE WEEKS after Kurnatovski's first visit, Anna Vassilievna, to Elena's great joy, returned to Moscow, to her large wooden house near the Prechistenka Boulevard—a house with pillars, white lyres and garlands over the windows, a wing, out-houses, a small garden, a big grass courtyard with a little well in it and a dog-kennel by the side of the well. Anna Vassilievna never left her summer residence as early as this, but she was suffering from a swollen cheek this year after the first cold spell of autumn. Nikolai Artemievich, on the other hand, having finished his "cure", missed his wife; Augustina Khristianovna, moreover, had gone to visit a cousin in Reval. Also a foreign troupe had arrived in Moscow with an exhibition of "poses plastiques", the description of which in the *Moscow Chronicle* had aroused Anna Vassilievna's curiosity. In a word, a prolonged stay out of town had become inconvenient and even, according to Nikolai Artemievich, incompatible with the fulfilment of his "designs".

The last two weeks had seemed very long to Elena. Kurnatovski came twice, two Sundays running, as he was busy during the week. He came really to see Elena, but talked more to Zoë, who found him very much to her liking. "Das ist ein Mann!" she thought to herself, watching his virile, sunburnt face and listening to his condescending, self-confident statements. In her opinion, there was no one with such a wonderful voice, no one who could enunciate so perfectly "I have the honour" or "I am extremely gratified".

Insarov did not come to the Stakhovs, but Elena saw him once in secret, in the small wood above the Moscow river, where they had arranged to meet. They hardly had time to exchange more than a few words.

Shubin returned to Moscow with Anna Vassilievna; Bersenev followed a few days later.

Insarov sat in his room and for the third time read through the letters brought to him from Bulgaria by hand, as his friends were afraid to send them by post. They caused him considerable anxiety. Events were developing rapidly in the East; the occupation of the Principalities by Russian troops exercised everybody's mind. The storm was blowing up; there was a feeling in the air that war was inevitable. The fire was kindling everywhere and no one could foresee where it would spread and where it would end. Old grievances, old hopes—everything was in a ferment. Insarov's heart was beating fast. His hopes, too, were on the point of fulfilment. "Is it not too early? Is it not in vain?" he thought to himself, clasping his hands. "We aren't ready yet. Still, if it must be, it must be. I'll have to go."

There was a faint sound on the other side of the door; it was pushed open and Elena walked into the room. Insarov, trembling all over, rushed to her, fell on his knees, clasped her in his arms and pressed his head to her heart.

"You didn't expect me?" she said quite out of breath (she had raced up the stairs). "Dearest, dearest!" She put both hands on his head and looked round the room. "So this is where you live! I found you very easily. Your landlord's daughter showed me the way. We moved back to town three days ago. I wanted to write to you, but thought that it would be better if I came. I can only stay a quarter of an hour. Get up and close the door."

He got up, quickly locked the door, came back to her and took her hands in his. He could not speak, for the joy he felt was choking him. She looked smilingly into his eyes —there was such happiness in them. She suddenly felt shy.

"Wait a moment," she said, gently pulling away her hands, "let me take off my hat." She untied the ribbons of her bonnet, pulled it off, slipped the cape from her shoulders, arranged her hair, and sat down on the narrow old sofa. Insarov did not move but watched her, spellbound.

"Sit down," she murmured, without raising her eyes to him and pointing to the seat beside her.

Insarov sat down, not on the sofa, but on the floor at her feet.

"Take off my gloves for me," she murmured in a faltering voice. She felt a little afraid.

He began to unbutton her glove, then to pull it off, but having pulled it only half off, he pressed his lips passionately against the soft and slender white hand that lay exposed. Elena gave a start and wanted to push him away with the other hand, but he began kissing it too. Elena drew it away, he threw back his head, she looked into his face, bent down . . . their lips met. . . . A moment passed . . . . She tore herself away, got up, whispered, "No, no!" and quickly moved towards the writing desk.

"Surely I'm the mistress here, and you can have no

secrets from me," she murmured, trying to appear at her ease, and standing with her back to him. "What a lot of papers! What are these letters?"

Insarov frowned. "Those letters?" he murmured, rising from the floor. "You can read them."

"There are so many of them and they're written in such small writing and I must go in a moment. . . . I won't bother! They aren't from a rival? Besides, they aren't in Russian," she added, turning the thin pages.

Insarov moved closer to her and put an arm round her waist. She suddenly turned to him, gave him a radiant smile and leaned on his shoulder.

"Those letters are from Bulgaria, Elena. My friends are writing and urging me to come."

"Now? Go there now?"

"Yes . . . now. While there is still time, while it's possible to get there."

She suddenly threw both arms round his neck. "You'll take me with you, won't you?"

He pressed her to his heart. "My dear, my dearest child, my heroine, how wonderfully you said that! But wouldn't it be wicked and mad of me—a homeless, lonely man—to take you with me? Take you where . . . ?"

She closed his lips. "Sh . . . or I'll be angry and never come to you again. As though everything hadn't long ago been decided and settled between us. As though I weren't your wife. Does a wife leave her husband?"

"Wives don't go to the wars," he murmured with a half-sad smile.

"No, not when they can stay behind. But can I stay behind here?"

"Elena, you're an angel . . . but only think of it, I may

have to leave Moscow in a fortnight. There can be no more dreaming for me of lectures at the University or of completing my studies. . . ."

"And what of that?" Elena interrupted. "You've got to go soon? All right, would you like me to stay with you now, this minute, stay for ever and not go home? Would you like that? Let's go now, shall we?"

Insarov pressed her to him with redoubled force. "May God punish me," he exclaimed, "if I'm doing wrong! From to-day we're together for life."

"Am I to stay here?" asked Elena.

"No, my precious treasure, no, my innocent child. You must go home to-day, but be ready. We can't do it so suddenly; we must think over everything carefully. We need money, passports."

"I've got some money," interrupted Elena, "I've got eighty roubles."

"Well, that's not much," remarked Insarov, "but it will be useful all the same."

"But I can find money, borrow some, ask Mamma— no, I won't ask her. But I can sell my watch . . . I have earrings, two bracelets, some lace. . . ."

"It's not the money that's the trouble, Elena, but what about your passport? How shall we get that?"

"Yes, how are we going to do that? Is it absolutely necessary to have a passport?"

"Absolutely."

Elena smiled. "Think what I've suddenly remembered! I was quite small at the time. . . . A maid of ours ran away. She was caught, forgiven, and lived with us for a long time, but everybody went on calling her Tatiana the Runaway.

I never thought then that I, too, might become a runaway like her.''

"Elena, how can you say such things?"

"Why not? Of course, it's better to go with a passport, but if we can't. . . ."

"We'll arrange it all in time, don't be in a hurry," murmured Insarov. "Let me think it over and see what can be done. We'll talk it all over together at leisure. And as to money, I have some too."

Elena stroked away the hair that had fallen over his forehead.

"Oh, Dmitri, how wonderful it will be to go together . . ."

"Yes," said Insarov, "but over there, where we're going. . . ."

"Well?" interrupted Elena, "isn't it also good to die together? And besides, why die? We will live, we're young. How old are you? Twenty-six?"

"Twenty-six."

"And I'm twenty. . . . Such heaps of time ahead. So you wanted to run away from me! No Russian love for the Bulgarian! I'd like to see you getting rid of me now! But what would have happened to us, if I hadn't gone to see you then. . . ."

"Elena, you know what made me go away then. . . ."

"I know, you fell in love and got frightened. But didn't you really know that I loved you?"

"I swear to you I didn't, Elena."

She bent forward suddenly and kissed him. "That is why I love you so. Now good-bye."

"Can't you stay any longer?" asked Insarov.

"No, dearest. Do you think it's easy for me to go? The

quarter of an hour was up long ago.'' She put on her cape and her hat. ''Come to us to-morrow evening. No, the day after to-morrow. It will be strained and boring, but never mind, at least we'll see each other. Good-bye. Let me out.''

He took her in his arms for the last time.

''Oh, you've broken my chain, you clumsy boy! Never mind. It's all for the best. I'll go to the Kusnetzki Bridge* and have it mended. If I'm asked any questions, I'll say I've been to the Kusnetzki Bridge.'' She touched the door-handle. ''Ah, I'd forgotten to tell you, Mr. Kurnatovski is probably going to propose one of these days. . . . But this is what I'll do to him.'' She put the thumb of her left hand to the tip of her nose and wiggled the other fingers in the air. ''Good-bye, au revoir. I know the way now. . . . And don't waste any time.''

Elena half-opened the door, listened, turned to Insarov, nodded and slipped out of the room.

Insarov stood for a moment in front of the closed door and also listened. The door below leading into the yard banged. He walked up to the sofa, sat down and covered his eyes with his hands. Nothing like this had ever happened to him before. ''How have I deserved such love?'' he thought. ''Is it a dream?''

But the subtle aroma of mignonette left by Elena in his dark and dingy room reminded him of her visit. The sound of her young voice, the patter of her light, young steps, the warmth, the freshness of her innocent young body still seemed to be there as well.

* Kusnetzki Bridge: the Moscow Bond Street—*Translator's note*

# CHAPTER XXIV

INSAROV DECIDED TO wait for more definite news, but began to prepare for his departure. It was a difficult business. As far as he was concerned, there were no obstacles, he merely had to apply for his passport; but what was he to do about Elena? It was impossible to get her a passport on legal grounds. Should he marry her in secret and then announce it to the parents? "They'd let us go, in that case," he thought. "And what if they refused? We'd go all the same. And what if they make a scandal, if. . . . No, better to try and get the passport in some way or other."

He decided to consult (naturally without giving any names) an acquaintance of his—a retired or disbarred lawyer, an old rogue experienced in dubious transactions. This estimable person lived some way away. Insarov, having spent a whole hour getting to him in a decrepit droshky, ended up by not finding him at home, and on the way back got drenched to the bone in a sudden downpour. The next morning, in spite of a bad headache, Insarov went again to see him. The lawyer listened to him carefully, sniffing snuff now and then from a snuffbox ornamented with the figure of a full-bosomed nymph, and stealthily watching his guest with his malicious little eyes, which were also the colour of snuff. Having heard his story, he asked for more "definite substance in the statement of

147

facts'' and, seeing that Insarov was reluctant to give any details (he had been loth to come in the first place) limited himself to the advice that he should first procure ''the needful'' and pay another visit, when, he added, sniffing from the open snuffbox, ''you will have armed yourself with more confidence and cast aside your suspicions.''

''As for the passport,'' he continued as though speaking to himself, ''that is simply a question of skill; once you're on your way, who on earth is going to know whether you are Maria Bredikhina or Karolina Vogelmeyer?''

A feeling of repugnance overcame Insarov, but he thanked the lawyer and promised to come back in a day or two.

That same evening he went to the Stakhovs. Anna Vassilievna gave him a warm welcome, reproached him for having forgotten them, and noticing that he was pale asked about his health. Nikolai Artemievich didn't say a word to him, only glanced at him casually, though with deliberate curiosity. Shubin gave him the cold shoulder. It was Elena, however, who surprised him. She was expecting him. She had put on specially for him the frock she had worn on the day of their first meeting in the chapel, yet she greeted him so calmly and was so easy, light-hearted and gay that, watching her, no one would have suspected that the fate of this girl was already ordained and that it was only the secret consciousness of happy love which animated her features and gave charm and ease to all her movements. She poured out the tea instead of Zoë, chattered away and joked. She knew that Shubin would be watching her, that Insarov would be unable to disguise his feelings—and had armed herself accordingly.

148

She was not mistaken. Shubin never took his eyes off her, and Insarov was very silent and glum the whole evening. Elena felt so happy that she couldn't resist the desire to tease him.

"Well," she asked him suddenly, "how is your plan progressing?"

Insarov was quite confused. "What plan?" he muttered.

"You've forgotten?" she replied, laughing in his face. (He alone could appreciate the meaning of that happy laughter.) "Why, the Bulgarian dictionary for Russians!"

"Quelle bourde!" Nikolai Artemievich muttered between his teeth.

Zoë sat down at the piano. Elena shrugged her shoulders slightly and motioned Insarov to the door, as though giving him leave to go. Then she tapped the table twice with her finger, very distinctly, and looked at him. He realized that she was fixing a meeting with him in two days time and she smiled swiftly when she saw that he had understood. Insarov got up and began saying good-bye. He was not feeling very well. Kurnatovski appeared. Nikolai Artemievich jumped up, raised his hand above his head and brought it down softly on the palm of the Secretary of the Senate. Insarov stayed on a few minutes in order to have a look at his rival. Elena gave him a sly, provocative nod—the host did not consider it necessary to introduce the two men to each other—and Insarov went away after exchanging a last look with Elena. Shubin became thoughtful for a while and then launched into a fierce discussion with Kurnatovski on a legal question about which he knew nothing.

Insarov did not sleep a wink the whole night and felt ill the next morning. He started, however, to put his papers in order and wrote some letters, though his head was heavy and somewhat confused. His temperature rose towards dinner time; he couldn't eat anything. Towards evening, the fever grew rapidly worse, his limbs ached and he had a splitting headache. Insarov lay down on the very sofa on which Elena had sat only a short while ago. He thought, "I've only myself to blame—why did I ever go to that old crook?" He tried to sleep. But the illness had already got a grip on him. The blood throbbed in his veins with a scorching, terrible force, his thoughts whirled in his head like a flock of birds. He lost consciousness. He lay on his back as if he had been knocked out, and suddenly he saw a vision—somebody laughing at him quietly and whispering. He made an effort to open his eyes; the light from the burning candle struck him painfully, like a knife. . . . What was that? It was the old lawyer in an Eastern dressing-gown, with a silk sash round the waist, as he had seen him the day before. "Karolina Vogelmeyer," whispered the toothless mouth. Insarov stared and the old man seemed to grow in length and breadth—he wasn't a man any more, but a tree; Insarov knew he must climb its twisted branches. He clung to them, then fell with his chest against a sharp stone, and Karolina Vogelmeyer was squatting on her haunches, dressed like a pedlar, muttering, "Pies, meat pies, pies,"—and further away there was blood flowing and the intolerable flash of swords. "Elena!" he cried, and everything vanished in a crimson whirl.

# CHAPTER XXV

"THERE'S A MAN here, can't think who he can be—a locksmith of sorts," announced Bersenev's servant the following evening. He was noted for his strict treatment of his master and for his sceptical turn of mind. "He says he wants to see you."

"Tell him to come in," said Bersenev.

The "locksmith" came in. Bersenev recognized him as the tailor, the landlord of the rooms where Insarov lived.

"Yes?" he asked.

"I've come to see your honour," began the tailor, slowly shuffling his feet and from time to time shooting out his right arm and clutching the cuff with three fingers. "Our lodger is very ill—who knows what may happen?"

"Insarov?"

"Yes, sir, our lodger. Who knows what may happen? Yesterday morning he was going about all right, in the evening he only asked for some water. The wife took him some and in the night he began to mutter away. We could hear him—there's only a thin partition between us—and to-day he doesn't say a word, just lies like a log, and the fever he's in—my God! I thought to myself, who knows what might happen, what if he died, God preserve us, hadn't I better advise the police? He's all alone, you see. But the wife says, 'Go to the gentleman our lodger stayed with in the summer, maybe he'll have something to say about it, or come himself.' So that's why I've come to your honour, because, after all, you know, we can't. . . ."

Bersenev seized his cap, pressed a rouble into the tailor's hand, and dashed with him to Insarov's rooms. He found him lying on the sofa, unconscious and fully dressed. His face had altered terribly. Bersenev told the landlord and landlady to undress him and carry him to bed. He himself rushed to fetch a doctor, and brought him back with him. The doctor prescribed leeches, mustard-plaster, calomel and blood-letting.

"Is he in danger?"

"Yes, very much so. Acute inflammation of the lungs, pneumonia in full swing. Maybe the brain is also affected, but he's a young man. At the moment his strength is against him. You were late calling me in, but we'll do, of course, all that science can do." The doctor was still young and believed in science.

Bersenev stayed the night. The landlord and landlady turned out to be kind and even efficient as soon as they had a man to tell them what to do. A male nurse arrived and then all the medical tortures began.

Towards morning Insarov recovered consciousness for a few minutes, recognized Bersenev, asked, "I believe I'm not well?", looked around with the listless, dull bewilderment of a very sick person, and relapsed into a coma. Bersenev went home, changed, took a few books with him and returned to Insarov's rooms. He had decided to stay with him at least for the time being. He put a screen round the bed and arranged a place for himself on the sofa. The day dragged on slowly and sadly. Bersenev only went out to get something to eat. Evening came. He lit the shaded candle and began to read. Everything around was still. Behind the partition he could hear the landlord's subdued whispering and an occasional yawn or sigh. Somebody sneezed and was reprimanded in a whisper. From behind the screen came the sound of heavy, uneven breathing, now and then interrupted by a short moan and a pathetic tossing of the head on the pillow. Strange thoughts assailed Bersenev. He was in the room of a man whose life hung by a thread and who—he knew it—was loved by Elena. . . . He remembered the night when Shubin had overtaken him and declared that she loved him—Bersenev. And now? "What shall I do now?" he asked himself. "Let Elena know about his illness? Or wait? This news will be more upsetting than what I had to tell her not so long ago. . . . It's odd how fate always makes me a go-between with them!"

He decided to wait. His eyes fell on the pile of papers on the table. . . . "Will he be able to fulfil his aspirations?" thought Bersenev, "or will they all fade away? He was filled with pity for this young life, ebbing away, and vowed to himself that he would try to save it.

Insarov had a bad night. He was delirious. Several times Bersenev got up from the sofa, approached the bed on tiptoe and listened anxiously to the disconnected ramblings. Only once did Insarov suddenly say quite clearly, "I don't want, I don't want . . . dearest, you mustn't. . . ." Bersenev started and glanced at Insarov: his face, deathly pale and drawn, was rigid and his arms lay limply on either side of his body. "I don't want . . ." he whispered half audibly.

The doctor came in the morning, shook his head and

prescribed new medicines. "He's still a long way from the crisis," he said, putting on his hat.

"And after the crisis?" asked Bersenev.

"After? There are two possibilities: *aut Caesar, aut nihil.*"

The doctor left. Bersenev walked up and down the street several times; he needed some fresh air. Then he came back and picked up a book. He had finished Raumer long ago and was now studying Grote. Suddenly the door squeaked softly and the head of the landlady's little daughter, wrapped, as usual, in a heavy shawl, peeped cautiously into the room.

"The young lady who gave me the ten copecks the other day is here . . ." she began in a whisper. Her head suddenly vanished and Elena appeared in its place. Bersenev jumped up as if something had stung him, but Elena did not move, did not utter a sound. She seemed to have taken it all in in a flash. A ghastly pallor suffused her face; she walked up to the screen, peered behind, clasped her hands in despair and stood as if turned to stone. Another moment and she would have rushed to Insarov's side, but Bersenev stopped her.

"What are you doing?" he murmured in an agitated whisper. "You might kill him."

She swayed. He led her to the sofa and made her sit down. She looked into his face, then looked him up and down, then stared at the floor.

"Is he dying?" she asked, so coldly and calmly that Bersenev was frightened.

"For God's sake, Elena Nikolaevna, what are you talking about?" he began. "He's ill, it's true, rather danger-ously ill; but we'll save him, I promise you we will."

"Is he unconscious?" she asked in the same voice.

"Yes, he's unconscious. . . . It always happens at the beginning of such illnesses, but it means nothing at all, I assure you. Drink some water."

She raised her eyes to him, and he realized that she hadn't heard his answer. "If he dies," she murmured always in the same voice, "I shall die too."

At that moment Insarov gave a slight moan. She shuddered, then snatched at her head and began to untie the ribbons of her bonnet.

"What are you doing?" Bersenev asked her.

She did not answer.

"What are you doing?" he repeated.

"I'm staying here."

"What . . . for some time?"

"I don't know, perhaps the whole day, the night, perhaps for ever . . . I don't know. . . ."

"For God's sake, Elena Nikolaevna, pull yourself together. I couldn't have expected to see you here, of course, but . . . but I presume, all the same . . . that you have just looked in for a short time. Remember that your absence will be noticed at home."

"Well, and . . . ?"

"They'll search for you . . . they'll find you. . . ."

"And what then?"

"Elena Nikolaevna! Don't you see . . . that he can't protect you at the moment?"

She lowered her head, as though deep in thought, put her handkerchief to her lips, and burst out into sudden convulsive sobbing that shook her whole frame. She threw herself on the sofa, burying her face in it to deafen the sound, but her body heaved and trembled like a bird caught in a snare.

"Elena Nikolaevna . . . for God's sake . . ." repeated Bersenev to her.

"Ah? What's that?" They suddenly heard Insarov's voice.

Elena dragged herself up, and Bersenev stood as though glued to the spot. After a pause, he went up to the bed. Insarov's head was as before, lying listlessly on the pillow; his eyes were closed.

"Is he delirious?" whispered Elena.

"I think so," replied Bersenev, "but that, too, doesn't mean anything—it's always the case, especially if. . . ."

"When did he fall ill?" asked Elena.

"The day before yesterday. I've been here since yesterday. You can rely on me, Elena Nikolaevna. Everything will be done. I won't leave him. If necessary we'll call in a second opinion."

"He will die without me . . ." she exclaimed, wringing her hands.

"I promise to let you have daily reports of the illness and should he really be in immediate danger. . . ."

"Swear that you'll send for me at once, no matter at what hour, day or night, send me a note direct . . . I don't care now what happens. Do you hear? Do you promise you'll do this?"

"I promise before God."

"Swear it."

"I swear."

She suddenly seized his hand and before he had had time to pull it away she pressed her lips to it.

"Elena Nikolaevna . . . what are you doing . . .?" he stammered.

"No, no, you mustn't . . ." Insarov muttered indistinctly, and gave a deep sigh. Elena walked up to the screen, stuffed her handkerchief between her teeth and looked for a long, long time at the sick man. Silent tears ran down her cheeks.

"Elena Nikolaevna," Bersenev said to her, "he may regain consciousness and recognize you, and God knows if that would be desirable. Also, I'm expecting the doctor any minute."

Elena took her hat from the sofa, put it on and stood still. Her eyes wandered sadly round the room. She seemed to be remembering. . . .

"I can't go away," she whispered at last.

Bersenev pressed her hand. "Try and be brave," he murmured, "don't worry, you're leaving him in my care. I'll come to see you this evening."

Elena glanced at him and whispered, "Oh, you dear kind friend!"—and, sobbing, ran out of the room.

Bersenev leant against the door. A bitter, painful emotion, yet not without a certain strange exaltation, constricted his heart. "You dear kind friend!" he thought and shrugged his shoulders.

"Who's there?" It was Insarov's voice.

Bersenev went up to him. "I'm here, Dmitri Nikanorovich. Is there anything you want? How do you feel?"

"Alone?" asked the sick man.

"Alone."

"And she?"

"Who do you mean?" murmured Bersenev half afraid. Insarov was silent.

"Mignonette," he whispered, and his eyes closed again.

# CHAPTER XXVI

FOR EIGHT DAYS Insarov lay between life and death. The doctor called constantly; as a young man he couldn't help being interested in a patient who was so dangerously ill. Shubin heard about Insarov's serious condition and came to see him. His compatriots also came, among whom Bersenev recognized the two strangers who had so surprised him by their unexpected visit in the summer. They all showed sincere sympathy, some of them offered to take turns with Bersenev at the bedside, but he refused, remembering his promise to Elena. He saw her every day and secretly communicated to her—sometimes by word of mouth, sometimes in a short note—the details of the illness. With what a faltering heart she waited for him! How she listened and questioned him! She was impatient to go and see him herself but Bersenev begged her not to. Insarov was seldom alone. The day after she first heard about his illness, she almost fell ill herself. Returning home, she shut herself up in her room, but she was summoned to dinner and arrived in the dining-room with such a face that Anna Vassilievna was alarmed and wanted to put her to bed. Elena managed however to control herself. "If he dies," she repeated to herself, "I shall die too." The thought of this reassured her and gave her the strength to appear indifferent. Besides, nobody bothered her. Anna Vassilievna was preoccupied with her swollen cheek. Shubin was working in a frenzy. Zoë had succumbed to melancholia and decided to read *Werther*. Nikolai Artemievich was annoyed by the frequent visits of the "scholar", all the more so because his "designs" with Kurnatovski were not progressing. The practical-minded Secretary was puzzled but patient.

Elena did not even thank Bersenev—there are services for which it is impossible and embarrassing to do so. Only once, on his fourth visit (Insarov had had a bad night and the doctor had suggested taking another opinion), only on that day did she remind him of his promise. "In that case, we'll go," he told her. She got up and was going to put on a coat. "No," he murmured, "let's wait till to-morrow." Towards evening Insarov took a turn for the better.

This ordeal went on for eight days. Elena seemed calm, but could eat nothing and did not sleep at night. She ached all over with a dull pain and a dry scorching smoke seemed to fill her head. "Our young lady is melting away like a candle," was how her maid put it.

At last, on the ninth day, the crisis came. Elena, barely conscious of what she was doing, was sitting in the drawing-room next to Anna Vassilievna, reading the *Moscow Chronicle* aloud to her. Bersenev came in. Elena glanced at him (how swift and timid, how anxious and penetrating was the first glance she gave him every time he came) and guessed at once that he was bringing good news. He smiled and nodded slightly. She got up to meet him.

"He's recovered consciousness, he's out of danger, he'll be well in a week," he whispered to her.

Elena stretched out her hands as though protecting

herself from a blow and did not say a word; only her lips trembled and a flush covered her cheeks. Bersenev started to speak to Anna Vassilievna and Elena went to her room, fell on her knees and began to pray and give thanks to God. Tears of relief glinted in her eyes. She suddenly felt very tired, put her head on the pillow, whispered, "Poor Andrei Petrovich" and went to sleep at once, her wet lashes touching her cheeks. She hadn't slept or cried for a long time.

# CHAPTER XXVII

BERSENEV'S WORDS ONLY partly came true—the danger passed, but Insarov recovered his strength very slowly and the doctor spoke of a deep and general undermining of his whole constitution. The patient, however, left his bed and walked about the room. Bersenev moved back to his own flat but came every day to see his friend, who was still very weak, and as usual kept Elena informed daily about his condition. Insarov did not dare write to her and only mentioned her casually in his talks with Bersenev, while the latter, with feigned indifference, told him about his visits to the Stakhovs, trying to make him understand, however, that Elena had been very much upset, but was calmer now. Elena did not write to him either. She had a better alternative in mind.

One day Bersenev, looking very cheerful, informed her that the doctor had at last allowed Insarov to have a cutlet and that he would probably soon be allowed out. She became thoughtful and looked down.

"Guess what I want to say to you," she murmured.

Bersenev was embarrassed. He knew what she meant. "You probably want to tell me that you would like to see him," he replied looking away.

Elena flushed and murmured almost inaudibly, "Yes."

"Well, it would be quite simple, I think." Ugh! What a horrible feeling there is in my heart! he thought.

"You mean that as I have already . . ." murmured Elena, ". . . but I'm afraid from what you say that he's seldom alone now."

"There'll be no difficulty about that," replied Bersenev, still not looking at her. "I can't warn him of your visit, of course, but give me a note. Who's to prevent you from writing to him—an old friend you're interested in? There could be no objection to that. Fix a day—that is, write and tell him when you think you will be able to go. . . ."

"I'm ashamed to," Elena whispered.

"Give me the note. I'll take it."

"No, that isn't necessary, but I wanted to ask you. . . . Don't be angry with me, Andrei Petrovich . . . don't go to see him to-morrow."

Bersenev bit his lip. "Ah! I see; very well, very well," he said, and after a few more words, he left her.

"It's better like that, it's better like that," he thought to himself as he hurried home. "It's not as if I didn't know it already, but it's better like that. What's the point of hanging on to another man's nest? I don't regret anything I've done. I did what my conscience told me, but now I'm through with it. So be it. My father was right when he said, 'You and me, my boy, are not sybarites, nor aristo crats; we've not been favoured by fate or nature, we're not even martyrs—we're just working men, working men, and working men. So on with your leather apron, and to your workman's bench in your dark workshop. Let the sun shine upon others. Even our obscure life has its pride and happiness."

The next morning Insarov received a short note by post: "Wait for me," wrote Elena, "and don't let in anybody else. A.P. is not coming to-day."

# CHAPTER XXVIII

INSAROV READ ELENA'S note, and instantly began to tidy up his room; he asked his landlady to remove the medicine bottles; took off his dressing-gown and put on a jacket. His head swam and his heart beat faster both from weakness and from joy. He did not feel very strong yet on his legs. He sat down on the sofa and began to watch the clock. "It's now a quarter to twelve," he told himself, "she can't come before twelve. I'll try to think of something else for a quarter of an hour, otherwise I shan't be able to bear it. She can't come before twelve. . . ."

The door burst open and Elena came in. She was wearing a light silk dress. She was pale, but she looked well and young and happy. With a faint cry of joy she fell on his breast.

"You're alive! You're mine!" she repeated, kissing him and stroking his hair. He hardly dared to breathe; he was overcome by her nearness, by her touch, by so much happiness.

She sat down by his side and nestled close to him and began to gaze at him with that laughing, caressing, tender look which is only seen in the eyes of a woman in love. A shadow fell across her face.

"How thin you've grown, my poor Dmitri," she said, stroking his cheek with her hand, "and what a beard you've got!"

164

"You've grown thin, too, my poor Elena," he replied, touching her fingers with his lips.

She shook out her hair light-heartedly. "Never mind. You'll see how we'll both recover! A storm broke out, like that day when we met in the chapel—it broke out and it has passed over. Now we're going to be alive!"

He answered her with a smile.

"What days they were, Dmitri, what cruel days! How do people go on living after the death of those they love? I always knew in advance what Andrei Petrovich was going to tell me; my life really seemed to ebb and flow with yours. And now my Dmitri has come back to me!"

He didn't know what to say to her. He wanted to throw himself at her feet.

"Another thing I noticed," she continued, smoothing back his hair—"I had plenty of time for noticing things in those days—when one is very, very unhappy, how foolishly absorbed one can become in one's surroundings! I assure you that I sometimes spent hours gazing at a fly, while my heart was absolutely chilled with fear. But all that is past, quite past, isn't it? Everything in the future will be happy, won't it?"

"You are my future," replied Insarov, "so it will be happy for me."

"And for me, too! D'you remember when I came to see you, not the last time, no, not the last time," she repeated with a shudder, "but when we were talking, I suddenly spoke of death, I don't know why, never thinking that it was round the corner. But now you're quite well, aren't you?"

"I'm much better, almost well."

"You're all right, you're alive. How happy I am!"

There was a short silence.

"Elena?" asked Insarov.

"Yes, my dearest?"

"Tell me, did it occur to you that this illness might have been sent to us as a punishment?"

Elena looked at him thoughtfully. "Yes, the idea did occur to me, Dmitri. But then I thought, why should I be punished? What crime had I committed, what duty had I neglected? Perhaps my conscience is not what some people's is, but it didn't reproach me. Perhaps it's against *you* that I've sinned. . . . I shall be a drag on you . . . get in your way."

"You won't, Elena, we'll go together."

"Yes, Dmitri, we'll go together. I'll follow you . . . that is my duty . . . I love you. I know of no other duty."

"Oh, Elena," murmured Insarov, "every word you say binds me to you indissolubly!"

"Why binds?" she asked. "We're both of us free. Yes," she went on, looking down thoughtfully, and continuing to stroke his hair with one hand, "I've gone through such a lot these last few days, such a lot, which I knew nothing about before. If anyone had told me that a carefully brought up young girl, like me, would run away from home under false pretences and go —where!—to a young man's rooms—how indignant I would have been! Yet that is what has happened and I don't feel any indignation. I really don't," she added, and turned to Insarov. He looked at her with such an expression of adoration, that she gently brought her hand from his hair to his eyes. "Dmitri," she began again, "you don't know it, but I saw you there, on that dreadful bed . . . I saw you in the grip of death, unconscious. . . ."

"You saw me?"

"Yes."

He was silent. "And Bersenev was here too?"

She nodded. Insarov bent over her. "Oh, Elena, I daren't look at you," he whispered.

"Why? Andrei Petrovich is so kind. I wasn't in the least embarrassed by him. Why should I be embarrassed? I'm quite prepared to tell the whole world that I'm yours. And I trust Andrei Petrovich like a brother."

"He saved me!" exclaimed Insarov. "He's the noblest, the kindest of men!"

"Yes     And d'you know that I owe everything to him? D'you know that he was the first to tell me that you loved me? And if only I could tell you all. . . . Yes, he's the noblest of men.

Insarov looked fixedly at Elena. "He's in love with you, isn't he?"

Elena lowered her eyes. "He loved me," she murmured under her breath.

Insarov pressed her hand tightly. "Oh, you Russians," he said, "what hearts of gold you have! And in spite of that he looked after me, spent sleepless nights. . . . And you, too, my angel . . . without a protest, without hesitation . . . and all this has come to me, to me. . . ."

"Yes, yes, to you, because you are loved. . . . Ah, Dmitri, how strange it all is! I believe I've told you that already—but never mind, I like repeating it and you won't mind hearing it again—when I saw you for the first time..."

"Why are there tears in your eyes?" Insarov interrupted her.

"Tears? Are there?" She wiped her eyes with a handkerchief. "You silly! You haven't discovered yet that one

167

can cry for happiness. Well, I was going to say, when I saw you for the first time I didn't see anything unusual in you, I really didn't. I remember that Shubin made a far greater impression on me, although I never loved him; and as for Andrei Petrovich . . . oh, there was a moment when I thought, can *he* be the one? But there was nothing like that with you. And then later . . . later . . . you just took away my heart with both hands. . . .''

"Don't . . .'' murmured Insarov. He wanted to get up, but sat down again at once.

"What's the matter?" Elena asked anxiously.

"Nothing . . . I'm still a bit weak . . . This happiness is more than I can stand yet.''

"Well, sit quietly. No movement, no excitement, if you please,'' she added, lifting a threatening finger. "And why did you take off your dressing-gown? It's too soon for monsieur to play the dandy. Sit down and I'll tell you some stories. Just listen and don't talk. It's bad for you to talk a lot after your illness.''

She began to tell him about Shubin, about Kurnatovski, about everything she had done during the past two weeks. She told him that war was inevitable, according to the papers, and that consequently, as soon as he was quite well again, they would have to find means of getting away, without losing a minute. . . . She said all this sitting next to him and leaning against his shoulder. He listened to her —listened, now growing pale, now flushing red, and several times tried to stop her. Suddenly he drew himself up.

"Elena,'' he said in a curiously harsh voice, "leave me, go away.''

"What?" she murmured in surprise. "Don't you feel well?" she asked quickly.

"No, I'm all right, but please go."

"I don't understand you. You're sending me away? . . . What are you doing?" she whispered suddenly as he bent down from the sofa to the floor and pressed his lips to her feet. "Don't do that, Dmitri . . . Dmitri. . . ."

He stood up. "Please go away! You see, Elena, when I fell ill I didn't lose consciousness at once. I knew that I was at death's door, even in my fever, in my delirium I understood, I vaguely felt that death was approaching. I was saying good-bye to life, to you, to everything. I was saying good-bye to hope. And then, suddenly, this resurrection, this light after darkness, you . . . you . . . so close to me, here with me, in the room . . . your voice, your breath . . . it's more than I can bear! I realize how passionately I love you, I hear you call yourself mine. . . . I can't control myself. Go away!"

"Dmitri," whispered Elena, and hid her head against his shoulder. She had only just understood what he meant.

"Elena," he continued, "I love you, you know that, I'm ready to give my life for you. . . . Why did you come now, when I'm weak, when I have no grip on myself? My heart is on fire, you tell me you're mine, that you love me. . . ."

"Dmitri," she repeated, and flushed and pressed more closely to him.

"Elena, have pity on me and go away. It's altogether too much for me. I can't resist this rush of passion. . . . I yearn for you with all my soul. . . . Only think, death almost parted us and now you are here in my arms . . . . Elena. . . ."

She trembled from head to foot. "Take me, take me, then," she whispered very faintly.

# CHAPTER XXIX

NIKOLAI ARTEMIEVICH STRODE up and down his study, frowning heavily. Shubin sat by the window, his legs crossed, calmly smoking a cigar.

"Do stop walking up and down like that," he muttered, tapping the ash off his cigar; "I keep on expecting you to say something and as I follow you with my eyes I get cramp in the neck. Besides, there's something strained and melodramatic in the way you're walking."

"All you do is play the fool," replied Nikolai Artemievich. "You don't wish to see my point, you won't realize that I've got used to this woman, that I'm attached to her, after all—that I'm miserable without her. Here we are in October, winter is almost here . . . what can she be doing in Reval?"

"Probably knitting stockings, for herself, not for you."

"You may well laugh . . . but I can tell you that I don't know a woman to equal her. Such honesty, such disinterestedness. . . ."

"Has she just presented a demand for payment?" asked Shubin.

"Such disinterestedness," repeated Nikolai Artemievich, raising his voice, "—it's wonderful! I'm told there are millions of other women in the world, but what I say is—show me these millions. Show me these millions, I say—ces femmes, qu'on me les montre!

And she doesn't write, that's what's so devastating!"

"You're as eloquent as Pythagoras," observed Shubin, "but do you know what I'd advise you to do?"

"What's that?"

"When Augustina Khristianovna returns . . . you understand me?"

"Well, yes . . . so what?"

"When you see her . . . do you follow me?"

"Yes, yes, I do."

"Try giving her a good spanking. See what happens then."

Nikolai Artemievich turned away, furious. "And I thought the fellow was really going to give me some good advice! But what can one expect from him! An artist, a man without 'standards'. . . ."

"Without standards . . . well, now, I hear that your favourite, Mr. Kurnatovski, a man *with* standards, took a hundred roubles in silver off you yesterday. That wasn't exactly delicate now, was it?"

"Well, we were playing for money. Of course, I might have expected. . . . But so little respect is shown him in this house. . . ."

"So he thought to himself—may as well take things as they come," continued Shubin; "whether he's to become my father-in-law or not is still in the lap of the gods, but a hundred roubles comes useful to a man who doesn't accept bribes."

"Father-in-law? What the devil do you mean! Vous rêvez, mon cher. Of course, any other girl would have jumped at such a fiancé. Judge for yourself: a bright and able man who has made his own way to success and done well in two districts. . . ."

"And led the governor in the V . . . . . . Government by the nose," remarked Shubin.

"Very probably. Must have deserved it. A practical business man. . . ."

"Good at cards," Shubin added.

"Yes, true, good at cards. But as for Elena Nikolaevna! Can anybody understand her? I'd like to see the man who could make out what she wants! One day she's gay, the next she's sad. She'll suddenly grow so thin that you can't bear looking at her, then suddenly she recovers—and all for no obvious reason. . . ."

An unprepossessing footman came in with a cup of coffee, a cream jug and a few biscuits on a tray.

"Her father approves of the fiancé," continued Nikolai Artemievich, brandishing a biscuit, "but does his daughter care a straw about that? In the old, patriarchal days it was all very well, but we've changed all that now. Nous avons changé tout cela. Nowadays young ladies talk with anybody they fancy, read anything they like, go to Moscow alone without a maid or a groom, as they do in Paris—and all this is considered comme il faut. A few days ago I asked, Where's Elena Nikolaevna? I was told that she'd gone out. Where? Nobody knew. Is that as it should be?"

"Take your cup and let the man go," muttered Shubin; "you're always saying pas devant les domestiques," he added in an undertone.

The footman glanced shiftily in his direction. Nikolai Artemievich took the cup, poured in some cream and scooped up about ten biscuits in his hand.

"What I wanted to say," he began as soon as the footman had gone, "is that I carry no weight in this house, that's all.

Because nowadays people only judge by appearances. A man can be empty-headed and stupid, but if he behaves as if he were important, he's respected. Another may have all the talents—talents which might possibly be of great use to humanity, but if he's modest. . . ."

"You're a born statesman, aren't you, Nikolinka?"* Shubin asked in a small, piping voice.

"Stop playing the fool!" Nikolai Artemievich exclaimed with irritation. "You forget yourself. There's another example for you that I have no authority in this house, none!"

"Anna Vassilievna tyrannizes you . . . you poor little thing," murmured Shubin, stretching himself. "Ah, Nikolai Artemievich, we ought to be ashamed of ourselves. You'd better try and find a little present for Anna Vassilievna, it's her birthday soon and you know how she values the slightest attention from you."

"Yes, yes," Nikolai Artemievich said hurriedly, "I'm glad you reminded me. Yes, yes, of course. . . . Why, I've got a nice thing right here, a jewelled clasp I got the other day at Rosenstrauchs, only I don't know if it'll be suitable."

"You bought it, I suppose, for the lady in Reval?"

"Well, I . . . I . . . thought. . . ."

"Well, in that case I'm sure it'll be suitable."

Shubin got up from his chair.

"Where shall we go to-night, Pavel Jakovlevich, eh?" asked Nikolai Artemievich, eyeing Shubin suggestively.

"Aren't you going to the Club?"

"But after the Club, after . . . ?"

* Diminutive of Nikolai.—*Translator's note.*

Shubin stretched himself again. "No, Nikolai Arte-mievich, I've got some work to do to-morrow. Some other time." And he walked out of the room.

Nikolai Artemievich looked sulky. He paced the room once or twice, took a velvet case out of the drawer and examined the piece of jewelry for some time, polishing it with a piece of silk. Then he sat down in front of the looking-glass and started carefully combing his thick black hair, tilting his face pompously now to the right, now to the left, pushing his tongue into his cheeks and keeping his eye on the parting.

Somebody coughed behind him. He turned round and saw the footman who had brought his coffee.

"What d'you want?" he asked.

"Nikolai Artemievich!" the footman enunciated, not without a certain solemnity; "you're our master!"

"Well, I know that and what else?"

"Nikolai Artemievich! Your honour must not be angry with me, but having been in the service of your honour's house since my early years, I feel it to be my duty as a zealous servant to inform your honour. . ."

"What are you talking about?"

The footman shifted uneasily. "Your honour," he began, "was saying he doesn't know where Elena Nikolaevna goes when she leaves the house. I have some knowledge of it."

"What are you lying for, you idiot!"

"As your honour pleases, but I did see her walk into a house four days ago."

"Which house? Where?"

"In the side-street near the Povarskaia. Not far from

here. I even asked the porter to tell me who the people are who live there.''

Nikolai Artemievich stamped his foot. ''Hold your tongue, you brute! How dare you! Elena Nikolaevna, out of the kindness of her heart, visits the poor and you. . . . Clear out, you idiot!''

The terrified footman hastened to the door.

''Stop!'' cried Nikolai Artemievich. ''What did the porter tell you?''

''No, nothing, your honour . . . just said a stu . . . a student.''

''Hold your tongue! Look here, you scoundrel, if I so much as hear that you've repeated this even in your sleep. . . .''

''How could I, your honour. . . .''

''Silence! If you so much as squeak . . . or if any one . . . if I learn . . . there won't be a corner left for you to hide in, even underground! Go! D'you hear?''

The footman vanished.

''God Almighty, what does this mean?'' thought Nikolai Artemievich, when he was alone again. ''What did that idiot say? Eh? I'll have to find out about that house and who lives there. . . . Go there myself. . . . This is a fine state of affairs! Un laquais! Quelle humiliation!'' And repeating loudly, ''un laquais!'', Nikolai Artemievich locked the piece of jewelry in the desk and went to see Anna Vassilievna. He found her in bed with a bandage round her jaw. But the sight of her sufferings only irritated him and he very soon reduced her to tears.

# CHAPTER XXX

MEANWHILE THE STORM that had been gathering in the East broke out. Turkey declared war on Russia; the time limit granted for the evacuation of the Principalities expired; the day of the massacre at Sinope was approaching.* The last letters Insarov received insisted on his returning home. He had not yet completely recovered; he coughed, was often overcome by fatigue or by a slight temperature, but he hardly ever stayed at home. His heart was aflame and he had no time now to think of his health. He drove about Moscow incessantly seeing various people in secret, wrote the whole night through, disappeared for whole days at a time. He informed his landlord that he would soon be leaving and made him a present in advance of all his modest furniture.

Elena, for her part, was also preparing to go. One cold and rainy evening she was sitting in her room, hemming handkerchiefs and listening with involuntary gloom to the howling of the wind. Her maid came in and told her that her father was in her mother's bedroom and wanted her to go there. "Your Mamma is crying," she whispered to Elena as she walked away, "and your Papa is in a dreadful temper."

* On 30 November, 1853, Vice-admiral Nakhimov destroyed a squadron of the Turkish fleet and reduced the town to ashes.— *Translator's note.*

Elena gave a shrug and went to Anna Vassilievna's bedroom. Nikolai Artemievich's better half was reclining in an easy chair, holding a handkerchief soaked with Eau-de-Cologne to her nose. He was standing by the fireplace, buttoned up to the neck, wearing a high, starched cravat and a stiff collar, vaguely reminiscent of a parliamentary speaker. With an eloquent gesture of his hand, he motioned his daughter to a chair and when she, misunderstanding the gesture, looked at him questioningly, he remarked with dignity, but without turning his head: "Please be seated." (Nikolai Artemievich was always ceremonious with his wife and with his daughter on special occasions.)

Elena sat down. Anna Vassilievna blew her nose tearfully. Nikolai Artemievich pushed his right hand under the lapel of his jacket.

"I sent for you, Elena Nikolaevna," he began after a long pause, "in order to ask you for an explanation, or, it would be better to say, to listen to your explanation. I am displeased with you . . . no, that is an understatement, your behaviour has upset and offended me—me and your mother . . . your mother, whom you see here. . . ."

Nikolai Artemievich brought only the bass notes of his voice into play. Elena looked at him in silence, then glanced at Anna Vassilievna, and turned pale.

"There was a time," Nikolai Artemievich began again, "when daughters did not permit themselves to despise their parents, when parental authority caused the disobedient to tremble. That time is no more, unfortunately —or anyway, so many people think. But believe me, that . . . that there are still some laws in existence that do not permit . . . do not permit . . . in one word, there are still some laws. I beg to draw your attention to this fact—there still exist some laws!''

''But Papa!'' Elena was on the point of saying.

''I must ask you not to interrupt me. Let us carry our minds back to the past. Anna Vassilievna and I have done our duty. Anna Vassilievna and I have spared nothing for your education, neither expense nor care. What profit you have derived from this care, this expense, is another matter, but I was entitled to presume, Anna Vassilievna and I were entitled to presume, that you would at least hold sacred those rules of morality that we . . . that we had inculcated in you, que nous vous avons inculqués in you, our only child. We had the right to think that no modern 'ideas' would find their way into this, shall we say, holy of holies. And what do we find? Without speaking of the foolishness characteristic of your sex, your age . . . who could have expected that you would so far forget yourself. . . .''

''Papa,'' murmured Elena, ''I know what you are talking about. . . .''

''No, you *don't* know what I'm talking about!'' Nikolai Artemievich shrieked in a high-pitched voice, suddenly abandoning the dignity of parliamentary behaviour, the suave pomposity of speech, and the bass notes. ''You don't know, you impudent girl . . . !''

''For God's sake, Nicolas,'' murmured Anna Vassilievna, ''vous me faites mourir. . . .''

''Don't tell me que je vous fais mourir, Anna Vassilievna! You couldn't even imagine what you are going to hear in a moment. Prepare yourself for the worst, let me tell you!''

Anna Vassilievna went numb all over.

"No," continued Nikolai Artemievich, turning to Elena, "you don't know what I'm going to say!"

"I feel very guilty towards you . . ." she began.

"Ah! At last!"

"I feel very guilty," went on Elena, "not to have told you before. . . ."

"Do you realize," Nikolai Artemievich interrupted her, "that I could ruin you with a single word?"

Elena looked up at him.

"Yes, young woman, with a single word . . . you needn't stare at me!" He crossed his arms over his chest. "May I enquire whether a certain house, in a side-street near the Povarskaia, is known to you? Have you visited it? (He stamped his foot.) Answer, you hussy, and don't think you can deceive me! People, servants, lacqueys, mademoiselle, de vils laquais, saw you go in, to see your . . ."

Elena flushed crimson and her eyes glittered.

"I have no desire to deceive you," she murmured. "I did go to that house."

"Splendid! D'you hear that, Anna Vassilievna? And you probably know who lives in it?"

"Yes, I do. My husband."

Nikolai Artemievich opened his eyes wide. "Your. . . ."

"My husband," repeated Elena, "I'm married to Dmitri Nikanorovich Insarov."

"You . . . married . . .?" Anna Vassilievna was hardly able to speak.

"Yes, Mamma, forgive me. . . . We were married secretly a fortnight ago."

Anna Vassilievna sank back into her chair. Nikolai Artemievich took two steps backwards. "Married! To this beggar, to a Montenegrin! The daughter of the nobleman,

Nikolai Stakhov, has married a commoner, a tramp! Without her parents' blessing! And you imagine I'll let matters stand where they are, that I won't raise a scandal! That I'll allow you to . . . to. . . . It's a convent for you and prison for him, a penal settlement! Anna Vassilievna, pray inform her at once that you disinherit her!''

"Nikolai Artemievich, for God's sake . . ." moaned Anna Vassilievna.

"And when and how did all this take place? Who married you? Where? My God, what will all our friends say, what will the world say! And you, you shameless dissembler, could go on living under your parents' roof, after such a deed . . . you weren't afraid of . . . a thunderbolt from heaven?''

"Papa," murmured Elena (she was trembling from head to foot, but her voice was steady), "you're at liberty to do what you will with me, but you're wrong to call me shameless and deceitful. I didn't want to . . . upset you before it was necessary, but I should have had to tell you about it one of these days anyway, because my husband and I are going away in a fortnight."

"Going away? Where to?''

"To his country. To Bulgaria."

"To the Turks!" exclaimed Anna Vassilievna, and fainted.

Elena rushed to her mother.

"Don't go near her!" yelled Nikolai Artemievich, seizing his daughter by the hand. "Keep away, you unworthy girl!''

But just then the bedroom door opened and revealed a pale face and a pair of flashing eyes. It was Shubin.

"Nikolai Artemievich!" he shouted as loudly as he

could, "Augustina Khristianovna has arrived and is asking for you!"

Nikolai Artemievich turned round in a fury, threatened Shubin with his fist, stopped for a moment, and rapidly left the room.

Elena fell at her mother's feet and clasped her knees.

Uvar Ivanovich was lying on his bed. A shirt without a collar but with a large stud in it encircled his fat neck, and fell in ample folds over his almost womanly breast, exposing a large cross of cypress wood and a small amulet. A light blanket covered his massive thighs. On the night-table, next to a mug of kvass, a candle burnt with a feeble flame and at the foot of the bed in a despondent attitude sat Shubin.

"Yes," he was saying thoughtfully, "she's married and preparing to go away. Your precious nephew yelled and bellowed enough to bring the house down, after shutting himself up in the bedroom for greater privacy; but not only the maids and footmen, but even the coachmen, could hear every word. He's raving and roaring even now; he almost went for me, flourishing his paternal curses like a bear with a sore head at a fair, but it won't get him any-where. Anna Vassilievna is distressed, but she's much more brokenhearted by her daughter's departure than by her marriage."

Uvar Ivanovich twiddled his fingers. "A mother . . ." he mumbled, "so . . . no wonder. . . ."

"Your nephew," continued Shubin, "threatens to go to the Metropolitan and to the Governor-General and to the Minister and lodge complaints, but it'll end by her going all the same. Who wants to ruin his own daughter? He'll kick up a fuss and cool down after a bit."

"They've . . . got no right . . ." remarked Uvar Ivanovich, and drank from his mug.

"That's so. And what a cloud of gossip, slander and criticism will rise in Moscow. She wasn't afraid of that . . . but she's above all that, of course. . . . She's going away and where! It makes one shudder to think! So far away, to so remote a place! What will she find there? To me it's as though she were leaving an inn in the middle of the night in a snowstorm, with 30 degrees below zero outside. She's giving up her country, her family—still, I understand her. What's she leaving behind here? Who's she going to miss? The Kurnatovskis and the Bersenevs and us, her humble servants? And these, after all, are the pick of the bunch. Why should she have any regrets? There's one bad thing, though. I'm told that her . . . husband—confound it, I can't bring myself to use the word!—I'm told that Insarov is spitting blood—that's a bad look-out. I saw him the other day: his face simply asking to be modelled as Brutus—d'you know who Brutus was, Uvar Ivanovich?"

"What's there to know? A man, presumably,"

"Exactly—a man. Yes, a wonderful face, but the face of a very sick person."

"For fighting—it's all one . . ." muttered Uvar Ivanovich.

"Yes, it's all one where fighting's concerned—you're almost making sense to-day—but what about living—and after all she wants to live with him."

"That's just youth . . ." said Uvar Ivanovich.

"Yes, youth—and a fine, brave thing it is. Death, life, struggle, defeat, victory, love, freedom, patriotism. . . . Fine, very fine. . . . God grant us all as much! It's different from sitting up to one's neck in a swamp and *pretending* that you don't mind it when, in fact, you *really* don't mind it. Over there, the strings are all keyed up—ready to vibrate for the whole world to hear—or else to break!''

Shubin let his head drop. ''Yes,'' he continued after a long pause, ''Insarov's worthy of her. No, what nonsense am I talking! Nobody is worthy of her. Insarov . . . Insarov. . . . Why this false modesty? Well, yes, he's a fine young man, able to stand up for himself, though up to now he's done nothing different from what all we poor mortals do; but are we such complete boors after all? Myself, for instance? Am I really such a boor, Uvar Ivanovich? Have I really been so badly treated by God? Did He give me no talents, no gifts? Who knows, maybe one day the name of Pavel Shubin will be famous? See that copper coin on the table? Who knows whether one day, in a century perhaps, this copper won't be used for a statue to Pavel Shubin, erected in his honour by a grateful posterity?''

Uvar Ivanovich leant on his elbow and stared at the excited artist.

''A remote hope that . . .'' he murmured at last, with the usual twiddling. ''You go on . . . all about yourself when we were talking of . . .''

''Oh, you great philosopher of all the Russias!'' exclaimed Shubin. ''Every word of yours is pure gold and it isn't to me, but to you, that a statue should be erected and I'll be the one to do it! Just in the pose you're in now, which might be either indolence or strength—one doesn't know—that's how I'll do you. I deserved that rebuke which showed up my egotism and conceit! You're right, of course, one shouldn't talk about oneself—there's nothing to boast of. There are no real men amongst us yet, none at all, no matter how far you look. Nothing but riff-raff, parasites, petty Hamlets; or boors, dunces and morons; or windbags, magpies and drivellers. And there's another kind, too: the people who've analysed themselves down to the last sordid detail and who constantly feel the pulse of every one of their emotions and then report to themselves: 'This is what I've just thought, this is what I've just felt.' A very profitable, useful occupation. No, if there had been some real men amongst us, this young girl, this sensitive spirit, would not have given us the slip like this. What shall we do, Uvar Ivanovich? When will our time come? When are we going to produce real men?"

"Give them time," answered Uvar Ivanovich; "they'll come."

"They will, you say? You—whom I see as an emblem of the Russian soil, as the force of its black earth! You say they'll come! Look out! I'm going to write those words down. Why are you blowing out the candle?"

"Want to sleep. Good-night."

# CHAPTER XXXI

WHAT SHUBIN SAID was true: the sudden news of Elena's marriage almost killed Anna Vassilievna. She took to her bed. Nikolai Artemievich had made her promise that she wouldn't admit her daughter into her presence. He seemed to be glad of the opportunity to prove that he was master in his own house, with all the authority of the head of the family. He roared and stormed at the servants the whole time, muttering continuously, "I'll show you what I can do, just you wait and see!" While he was at home, Anna Vassilievna did not see Elena and had to be content with Zoë, who waited on her most attentively but thought to herself, "Diesen Insarov vorziehen—und wem?" But as soon as Nikolai Artemievich left the house (and that was frequently because Augustina Khristianovna had at last returned) Elena went to see her mother, who gazed at her for a long time in silence, with tears in her eyes. Her silent reproach cut deeper into Elena's heart than any other. She did not feel any remorse at the time, only a deep and infinite sadness akin to remorse.

"Mamma, dearest Mamma!" she said repeatedly, kissing her hands. "What else could I do? I'm not to blame, I love him, I couldn't have behaved differently. It's fate you ought to blame for having brought me together with a man Papa doesn't like and who is taking me away from you."

G

"Oh!" Anna Vassilievna interrupted her, "don't remind me of that. When I think of where you propose to go, my heart sinks. . . ."

"Dearest Mamma," replied Elena, "try and console yourself with the thought that it might have been worse, that I might have died. . . ."

"Anyway, I don't expect ever to see you again. Either you'll end your days somewhere there in a tent (Anna Vassilievna visualised Bulgaria as a sort of Siberian tundra) or I'll not survive the parting. . . ."

"Don't say that, dear Mamma, God grant we shall see each other again. And there are towns in Bulgaria, like there are here."

"Towns? What towns can there be? There's a war there now, I expect guns are shooting wherever you go. . . . When do you want to start?"

"Very soon . . . if only Papa . . . he says he's going to create a scandal, he wants to separate us. . . ."

Anna Vassilievna raised her eyes to the ceiling. "No, Lenochka, he won't create a scandal. I would never have agreed to this marriage myself, I'd have sooner died, but what's done can't be undone and I'm not going to let anyone ruin my daughter."

A few days went by. At last Anna Vassilievna summoned all her courage and one evening shut herself up in her bedroom alone with her husband. The house became tense and still. At first nothing could be heard, then came the loud drone of Nikolai Artemievich's voice; they could be heard arguing, then shouting, and every now and then there was something that sounded like a moan. Shubin, along with the maids and Zoë, was already preparing to go to the rescue, when the noise in the bedroom began to subside, turned into ordinary conversation and faded away altogether. One could only hear faint sniffing from time to time and soon even that stopped. Then came the jingle of keys, the creak of the desk being undone. . . . The door opened and Nikolai Artemievich appeared. He looked sternly at everybody he saw and went off to his club. Anna Vassilievna sent for Elena, threw her arms around her and, crying bitterly, murmured, "It's all arranged, he won't make any fuss . . . and there's nothing now to prevent you from going . . . and leaving us."

"Will you allow Dmitri to come and thank you?" Elena asked her mother as soon as she had calmed down a little.

"Wait a little, my dear, I can't bear yet to see the man who's taking you away. . . . We'll have time to do it before you go."

"Before we go . . ." Elena repeated sadly.

Nikolai Artemievich had agreed "not to make a fuss", but Anna Vassilievna did not tell her daughter at what a price. She didn't tell her that she had had to promise to pay all his debts and had given him a thousand roubles in cash. Moreover, he had told Anna Vassilievna that he refused to see Insarov, whom he continued to call the Montenegrin. On reaching his club he began without any particular prompting to talk to his partner, a retired General of Infantry, about Elena's marriage. "Have you heard," he remarked with feigned indifference, "that my daughter, because she's had too much education, has married a student of sorts?" The general looked at him through his spectacles, grunted—"Hm . . ."—and asked what were trumps.

# CHAPTER XXXII

THE DAY OF their departure was now approaching. November was drawing to a close. All the time limits had expired. Insarov had completed his preparations and was burning with the desire to leave Moscow as soon as possible. The doctor, too, kept urging him to go. "You need a warm climate," he told him; "you won't really get better here."

Elena, too, was impatient to go. Insarov's paleness, his thinness, filled her with anxiety. She often studied his altered features anxiously. The situation at home had become unbearable. Her mother pronounced litanies over her as though she were already dead, her father treated her with cold contempt. The approaching separation tormented him, too, at heart, but he considered it his duty, the duty of an offended parent, to hide his feelings, his weakness. Anna Vassilievna at last expressed a wish to see Insarov. He was brought in secretly by the back entrance. When he walked into her room, she was unable at first to utter a sound and could not bring herself to look at him. He sat down by the side of her chair, calmly and respectfully, and waited for her to say the first word. Elena was also sitting there, holding her mother's hand in her own. Anna Vassilievna at last raised her eyes, murmured, "God be your judge, Dmitri Nikanorovich," and broke off. All further reproaches remained on her lips unspoken. "But you're ill!" she exclaimed. "Elena, he's ill! You've got a sick man here."

"I have been ill, Anna Vassilievna," replied Insarov, "and I haven't quite recovered yet . . . but I hope that the air of my country will make me well again."

"Yes, Bulgaria!" whispered Anna Vassilievna, and thought to herself, "Good God, a Bulgarian, a dying man —with a voice as hollow as if it came out of a barrel and eyes like bulbs; a real skeleton; a suit that looks as though it belonged to someone else—yellow as a dandelion—and she's his wife, she loves him—it's like a bad dream. . . ." But she pulled herself together at once.

"Dmitri Nikanorovich," she murmured, "you're sure you must go, you really must go?"

"I must, Anna Vassilievna."

Anna Vassilievna looked at him. "Oh, Dmitri Nikanorovich, may God spare you from ever having to go through what I'm going through now. . . . But promise me that you will love and cherish her. . . . You won't have to trouble about money while I'm alive. . . ." Tears choked her voice. She threw her arms out to them and enfolded Elena and Insarov in her embrace.

The fateful day had come at last. It was decided that Elena should say good-bye to her parents at home and set off on the journey from Insarov's rooms. The departure was fixed for midday. Bersenev turned up a quarter of an hour before the appointed time. He expected to find the Bulgarians at Insarov's rooms, waiting to see him off, but they had already left, along with the two mysterious figures (known to the reader) who had been witnesses at Insarov's marriage. The tailor greeted "the worthy master" with a deep bow; in his grief—or was it joy because of the furniture he'd acquired?—he had got very drunk. His wife soon led him away. Everything was already tidied away in the room; the trunk, with a strap round it, stood on the floor. Bersenev became thoughtful—his mind was full of memories.

Twelve o'clock had struck long ago and the coachman had brought round the horses, but the "newly-weds" did not appear. At last hurried footsteps were heard on the stairs and Elena appeared, accompanied by Insarov and Shubin. Elena's eyes were red. She had left her mother in a dead faint. The parting had been very painful. Elena hadn't seen Bersenev for more than a week. He had seen little of the Stakhovs lately. She had not expected to see him and cried out: "You! Oh thank you for coming!" and threw herself on his neck. Insarov also embraced him. There was a painful silence. What could these three people say to one another? What were the three of them feeling in their hearts? Shubin saw that it was essential to relieve the tension, by a sound, by a word.

"Here's our trio," he began, "together once again—and for the last time. Let us submit ourselves to the decrees of fate; let us remember the past with gratitude, and look forward to blessings in the future." He began to sing, "God be with us on our new road," and then stopped. He was suddenly ashamed and embarrassed. It is unseemly to sing when there is a dead body in the room and at that moment and in that room, the past he had mentioned was already dead—the past of those who were gathered there. True, it had died to give birth to a new life, but it was dead all the same.

"Well, Elena," Insarov began, turning to his wife,

"that's all, I think? Everything paid and packed. Only the trunk to take down. Heh! Landlord!"

The landlord walked into the room with his wife and child. He listened, swaying slightly on his feet, to Insarov's orders, threw the trunk over his shoulder and ran swiftly down the stairs, clattering his heels as he went.

"Now, according to Russian custom, we ought to sit down," remarked Insarov.

Everybody sat down—Bersenev on the little old sofa, Elena next to him, while the landlady and her daughter squatted in the doorway. They were all silent. There were strained smiles on every face, though none of them knew why they were smiling; each of them wanted to say something before parting, but each (except, of course, the landlady and her daughter, who merely gaped) felt that on such occasions all one could do was to utter a platitude, because a significant, intelligent or merely a sympathetic word would seem inadequate, even insincere.

Insarov was the first to get up. He made the sign of the Cross. "Good-bye to our little room!" he exclaimed. This was followed by kisses—the loud but formal kisses of farewell—the final, unspoken wishes, the promises to write, the last half-stifled good-byes.

Elena, bathed in tears, was already getting into the sleigh. Insarov, full of solicitude, was covering her knees with a rug. Shubin, Bersenev, the landlord, his wife and daughter with the eternal shawl on her head, the door-keeper, a casual workman in a striped smock, were all standing by the porch, when a luxurious sleigh, drawn by a dashing trotter, swept into the yard and Nikolai Arte-mievich, shaking the snow off the collar of his cloak, jumped out of it.

"In time, after all, thank God!" he exclaimed, and rushed up to the other sleigh. "Here, Elena, is our last paternal blessing," he said, and pulling out a small ikon in a velvet bag hung it round her neck. She burst into tears and started kissing his hands, while the coachman took out of the front part of the sleigh a half-bottle of champagne and three glasses.

"Well, now!" said Nikolai Artemievich, and tears streamed down the beaver collar of his cloak. "We must see you off and wish you. . . ." He began pouring out the champagne but his hands trembled and the foam rose above the brim and fell on the snow. He took one glass and gave the other two to Elena and Insarov, who had already taken his seat at her side. "May God . . ." began Nikolai Artemievich, and could not go on. He drank the wine and they drank too. "Now it's your turn, gentlemen," he added, turning to Bersenev and Shubin, but at that moment the coachman started the horses. Nikolai Artemievich ran by the side of the sleigh. "Don't forget to write!" he panted. Elena leant out, murmuring, "Good-bye, Papa. Good-bye, Andrei Petrovich, Pavel Jakovlevich, good-bye, Russia," and fell back on to the seat. The coachman raised his whip and whistled; the sleigh, screeching on its runners, turned to the right outside the gate and disappeared.

# CHAPTER XXXIII

IT WAS A clear April day. A peaked gondola was gliding over the broad lagoon that separates Venice from the narrow strip of exposed sand, called the Lido. It rocked gently at each thrust of the long pole the gondolier was leaning against. Under its low little awning, on soft leather cushions, sat Elena and Insarov.

Elena's features had not changed much since her departure from Moscow, but her expression had altered. It was more serious, more reflective, and there was a more assured look in her eyes. Her whole body had blossomed out and her hair seemed thicker and more luxuriant above the white forehead and fresh cheeks. Only round the lips, when she was not smiling, a barely noticeable wrinkle revealed the presence of a constant, secret preoccupation. With Insarov it was exactly the opposite—his expression was the same, but his features had undergone a cruel change. He had grown thin and old, he was pale, he stooped, he coughed almost incessantly with a short, dry cough, and his sunken eyes gleamed with a strange fire. On the way from Russia, Insarov had been laid up for almost two months in Vienna, and it was only at the end of March that he and his wife had reached Venice; from there he hoped to make his way through Zara into Serbia and Bulgaria, alternative routes being closed to him. War was already raging along the Danube. England and France had

G*                          193

declared war on Russia. All the Slav countries were in a ferment and getting ready for revolution.

The gondola approached the inner shore of the Lido. Elena and Insarov made their way along a narrow sandy track bordered by stunted little trees (they are planted every year and every year they die) towards the outer shore of the Lido and the sea. They walked along the fore-shore. The faded blue waters of the Adriatic surged in front of them; foaming and hissing, they raced towards the shore and, as they withdrew, left small shells on the sand and fragments of sea-weed.

"What a gloomy place!" remarked Elena. "I'm afraid it's too cold for you here, but I think I know why you wanted to come."

"Cold?" retorted Insarov with a quick but bitter smile; "I shall be a fine soldier if I'm going to be afraid of the cold. Why did I come here? I'll tell you why. I gaze at the sea here and it seems to me that I'm closer to my country. For it's just over there," he added, pointing to the East, "and the wind is blowing from there."

"Perhaps this wind will bring the ship you're waiting for?" said Elena, "Look at that white sail. Isn't that it?"

Insarov looked at the vast expanse of water to which Elena was pointing.

"Rendich promised to arrange everything in a week," he remarked, "I believe I can rely on him. . . . Did you hear, Elena," he added with a sudden wave of enthusiasm, "that the poor Dalmatian fishermen have given all their drag-weights—you know, the ones with which nets are thrown to the bottom of the sea—for bullets? They've no money—they earn their living by fishing—but they gladly gave their only belongings and now face starvation. What a people!"

"Aufgepasst!" a haughty voice called out behind them. The dull thud of horses' hooves was heard, and an Austrian officer in a short grey tunic and green cap galloped past them. They had barely time to step aside. Insarov looked after him with a sullen frown.

"He isn't to blame," murmured Elena. "You know they've no other place here where they can ride their horses."

"He isn't to blame!" retorted Insarov, "but he's made my blood boil with his shouting and his moustache, and his cap—his whole appearance. Let's go home."

"Yes, let's, Dmitri. Besides, it's really blowing hard here. You weren't careful enough after your Moscow illness and you paid for it in Vienna. You must be more careful now."

Insarov remained silent, but the same bitter smile hovered on his lips.

"Would you like to take a trip on the Grand Canal?" continued Elena. "We haven't really seen anything of Venice since we arrived. And in the evening we'll go to the theatre. I've got two seats in a box. I'm told they're giving a new opera. Shall we devote this day to ourselves, forget about politics, about the war, about everything and only remember one thing—that we're alive, that we breathe, that we think alike, that we're joined for ever. . . . Shall we do that?"

"If you want to, Elena," replied Insarov, "it means that I want to, too."

"I thought so," Elena remarked with a smile. "Come on, let's go."

They returned to the gondola, got into it and asked to be taken slowly along the Grand Canal.

Those who have never seen Venice in April do not really know the inexpressible charm of that magic city. The softness and mellowness of spring suits Venice, just as the dazzling summer sun suits the magnificence of Genoa, and the gold and purple of autumn becomes the grandeur and antiquity of Rome. The beauty of Venice, like the Spring, moves one and stirs up desire. Venice fills the inexperienced heart with longings and tantalizes it with the promise of immediate, unequivocal, yet mysterious happiness. Everything about her is limpid, clear and at the same time enveloped in the misty spell of an enchanted stillness; everything about her is withdrawn and at the same time inviting; everything about her is feminine, beginning with her name, for it is not in vain that she alone of cities has been called Beautiful—*La Bella*. Her lofty palaces and churches stand shimmering and superb, the perfect vision of some young immortal. In the absence of street noises, the harsh clatter, din and hubbub of urban life, there is something supernatural, something strangely attractive in the glaucous, silky surface of the muffled waves in her canals, and the noiseless passage of her gondolas.

"Venice is dying, Venice is deserted," her inhabitants tell you, but was it not just this last enchantment perhaps, the charm of decay which was wanting in the full bloom and triumph of her beauty? Those who have not seen her do not know her; neither Canaletto, nor Guardi (not to mention modern artists) was capable of rendering the silvery delicacy of the atmosphere, the remoteness and nearness of the sky, the wonderful harmony of her graceful outlines and blending colours. To one who has had his day or to whom life has been unkind, Venice has nothing to offer; she will make him wince by reminding him of the unfulfilled dreams of youth; but she will respond to one who is full of vigour and whose mind is at peace. Let such a one surrender his happiness to her bewitching skies and however radiant it may be she will enrich it still more with an imperishable intensity.

The gondola in which Insarov and Elena were sitting slowly passed the Riva degli Schiavoni, the Palace of the Doges, the Piazzetta, and entered the Grand Canal. The marble palaces stretched away on both sides. They seemed to be slowly floating past, without giving the eye time to take in and understand all their beauty. Elena felt profoundly happy. There was only one tiny cloud in her sky and even that had disappeared—Insarov was feeling much better that day. They glided up to the steep arch of the Rialto bridge and turned back. Elena feared the cold of the churches for Insarov, but she remembered the Accademia di Belle Arti, and told the gondolier to go there. Before long they had walked through all the rooms of this small gallery. Being neither experts, nor amateurs, they did not stop in front of every picture, did not drive themselves; they felt unexpectedly light-hearted. Everything suddenly seemed to amuse them. (Children know what it is to feel like this.) To the great indignation of three English tourists, Elena laughed till she cried over Tintoretto's St. Mark, jumping from heaven like a frog into water to prevent a slave being tortured. Insarov was carried away by the sight of the back and calves of the powerful man in a green cape who stands in the foreground of Titian's *Assumption of the Virgin* and stretches out his hands to the Madonna; the Madonna herself, a strong and beautiful woman, calmly and solemnly striving to be embraced by God the Father, struck both Insarov's and Elena's fancy; they also enjoyed the sombre sacred painting by old Cima da Conegliano.* As they left the Accademia, they turned round for another look at the Englishmen, with their rabbit teeth and drooping side whiskers, who were walking behind them—and laughed; they saw their gondolier in a skimpy jacket and shorts—and laughed; they noticed a pedlar with a knob of grey hair on the very top of her head—and laughed even more; they looked straight into each other's faces and burst into peals of laughter, and as soon as they were in the gondola again, they held each other's hands tightly.

They reached their hotel, ran to their room and ordered dinner to be sent up to them. Their merriness did not leave them at table either. They kept urging each other to eat; drank to the health of their friends in Moscow; commended the cameriere for a delicious fish course and asked him to show them some live frutti di mare; the cameriere shuffled with his feet and fidgeted and, leaving the room, shook his head and once even whispered with a sigh, "Poveretti!"

After dinner they went to the theatre. They were giving a Verdi opera—a rather commonplace one, to tell the truth, but one that had already made the round of all the opera-houses in Europe and was well-known in Russia too —*La Traviata*. The season in Venice was over and the singers did not rise above the level of mediocrity. They all

* Of the Madonna enthroned, with saints and angels making music.—*Translator's note.*

shouted as loud as their lungs could manage. Violetta's part was sung by a little-known artiste who, to judge by the coldness of her reception, was not a popular favourite, though she was not without talent. She was a dark-eyed girl, young and not particularly beautiful, with an uneven and already tired voice. She was dressed in ridiculously gaudy, ugly clothes with a red net over her hair. Her dress, which was made of faded blue satin, was too tight over her bosom, and her thick suede gloves came up to her bony elbows. Yes, how was she, the daughter of some obscure shepherd from Bergamo, to know how the "Dames aux Camélias" of Paris dressed? Nor did she know how to move about the stage, though there was a good deal of sincerity and guileless simplicity in her acting and she sang with the peculiar passion of expression and rhythm which only Italians can achieve.

Elena and Insarov sat alone in the dark box, very close to the stage. They were still in the frivolous mood that had overcome them in the Accademia di Belle Arti. When the father of the unfortunate youth, who falls into the toils of the seductress, appeared on the stage in a pea-coloured frock-coat and dishevelled white wig, opened his mouth crookedly and, obviously uncertain of the effect, emitted a dismal bass tremolo, they both almost burst out laughing. Violetta's acting, however, impressed them.

"That poor girl gets so little applause," said Elena, "yet I prefer her a thousand times to some self-confident, second-rate celebrity, who would be affected, pretentious and give herself airs. This one seems to take it very seriously—you can see she's not even aware of the audience."

Insarov leant on the edge of the box and looked intently at Violetta.

"Yes," he murmured, "it's no joke in her case—there's a kind of odour of death about her."

Elena was silent.

The third act began. The curtain went up. Elena felt herself shudder at the sight of the bed, the drawn curtains, the medicine bottles, the shaded light. She recalled the not so distant past. "And the future? The present?" flashed through her brain. As though on purpose, the actress's feigned cough was answered from the box by Insarov's hoarse and genuine one. Elena glanced at him out of the corner of her eye, and her face immediately assumed a calm and unconcerned expression. Insarov, who understood what she meant, smiled and began softly to join in the singing. Very soon, however, he was silent again. Violetta's acting improved all the time, became more uninhibited. She discarded everything unessential and superfluous, and found herself—a rare, a sublime happiness for an artist. She had suddenly crossed the frontier line which it is impossible to define, but beyond which beauty dwells. The audience held its breath in surprise. The ungainly girl with the tired voice had begun to control it, to dominate it. But her voice did not sound tired any more; it had warmed up, had gained strength. When Alfredo appeared, Violetta's cry of joy almost provoked the storm, which the Italians call *fanatismo*, and compared with which our restrained applause is nothing at all. . . . Another moment and the audience became spellbound again. It was the duet, the best moment of the opera, in which the composer succeeded in expressing all the regrets of misspent and foolish youth, the dying struggle of desperate and hopeless love. Carried away, transported by the wave of general sympathy, with tears of joy and real suffering in her eyes, the singer surrendered to the wave that was lifting her, her face became transformed and as the grim phantom of rapidly approaching death confronted her, the words—"Lascia mi vivere . . . morir si giovane . . ."—were torn from her in a prayer of such passionate appeal to divine mercy that the whole theatre shook with frenzied applause and rapturous cries.

Elena felt quite numb. She began searching gently for Insarov's hand and squeezed it tightly. He responded with the same pressure, but she did not look at him, nor he at her. This pressure of their hands now meant something different from what it had a few hours earlier in the gondola.

They glided back again to their hotel on the Grand Canal. Night had fallen, a bright and balmy one. The same palaces stretched out in front of them, but they seemed different. Those of them that were lit by the moon had a pale golden sheen in which the details of ornamentation and the outlines of windows and balconies seemed to vanish; they stood out more distinctly on those buildings which were lightly wrapped in shadow. The gondolas with their little red lights seemed to glide more swiftly and noiselessly than ever, their steel prows glittered mysteriously, the oars rose and fell mysteriously among the silver scales of the ruffled water; apart from the sporadic muffled cries of the gondoliers, who never sing nowadays, there was scarcely a sound to be heard.

The hotel where Insarov and Elena were staying was on the Riva degli Schiavoni. They got out of the gondola before reaching it and walked several times round the

Piazza di San Marco. Under the colonnades crowds of idle people had collected in front of the small cafés. There is a peculiar fascination in walking about among strangers in a strange town with somebody one loves—everything seems beautiful and significant and one cannot help wanting everyone else to share one's own peace, serenity and happiness. But Elena was no longer able to surrender light-heartedly to her own happiness; her heart, shaken by recent impressions, could not recover its calm and as they passed the Palace of the Doges, Insarov pointed, without comment, to the Austrian guns poking out of the base-ment, and pulled his hat down lower over his forehead. Besides, he felt tired; and, with a last glance at St. Mark's and its domes, the bluish lead of which gleamed in the moonlight with a phosphorescent glow, they slowly wandered back to their hotel.

Their little room looked out over the wide lagoon that spreads from the Riva degli Schiavoni to the Giudecca. Almost directly opposite the hotel rose the spear-headed tower of San Giorgio Maggiore; to the right, high up in the air, glittered the golden dome of the Dogana; and, arrayed like a bride—most beautiful of churches—Palladio's Redentore. On the left were silhouetted the dark outlines of ships' masts and yard-arms, the funnels of steamers, and an occasional half-folded sail hanging like a large wing among the almost motionless rigging.

Insarov sat down by the window, but Elena would not let him admire the view for long. He suddenly felt feverish and overcome by weakness. She put him to bed and, after waiting for him to go to sleep, returned silently to the window. What a mild and gentle night it was—blue as lapis lazuli and as soft as a dove. Surely, it seemed to her, all pain and sorrow must be stilled and assuaged beneath this limpid sky, and under the moon's benign and purifying influence.

"Oh God," thought Elena, "why should there be such things as death and parting and illness and tears—why, on the other hand, this loveliness, this blissful feeling of hope, the reassuring sense of a secure shelter, of unfailing protection, of eternal guardianship? What does it all mean— this smiling, friendly sky, this calm and happy earth? Is it possible that it's only inside ourselves after all and that outside there is nothing but eternal cold and silence? Is it possible that here we are alone—alone—and that up there, in the unfathomable depths and abysses of space, everything is hostile to us? If so, why is it that we long for prayer and for the relief it brings? ("Morir si giovane" echoed in her heart.) Was it impossible to ward of danger, to have one's prayers answered? Oh God, was it after all then impossible to believe in miracles?"

She rested her head on her folded hands. "Enough?" she whispered, "have I really had enough? I've been happy, not only for minutes, for hours, for days, but for weeks on end I've been happy. And by what right?" She felt frightened by her happiness. "What if it can't go on?" she thought; "if it can only be had at a price? We've been in heaven, after all, and we're only human beings, poor, sinful human beings. "Morir si giovane. . . ." Haunt me no more, dark phantom! It's not only for my sake that he must live. But what if this is our punishment?" she thought again; "what if we now have to settle in full for the wrong we have done? My conscience was silent, is silent even now, but is this a proof of innocence? Oh God, are we in truth such sinners! Thou who hast created this sky, this night, is it Thy will to punish us for having loved? And if it is, if he is guilty, if I am guilty . . ." she added with a sudden outburst, "—Oh, then, Oh God, grant that we should both die at least an honourable and glorious death, over there, on his native soil, not here in this obscure room. . . ."

"And what of the grief of my poor lonely mother?" she asked herself, and became confused and found no answer to her question. Elena did not realize that the happiness of one involves the misery of another, that even one person's prosperity and comfort requires—as a statue requires a pedestal—the disadvantage and discomfort of others.

"Rendich!" Insarov murmured in his sleep.

Elena approached him on tiptoe, bent over him and wiped the perspiration from his forehead. He tossed a little on his pillow and was quiet again. She returned to the window and her thoughts again assailed her. She began to persuade herself, to reassure herself that there was no ground for alarm. She was even ashamed of her apprehensiveness.

"Is he really in danger? Isn't he much better?" she whispered. "If we hadn't been to the theatre this evening, none of this would have occurred to me."

At this moment, she saw a white sea-gull flying high over the water. It had probably been startled by a fisherman and flew noiselessly, with an uneven flight, as though looking for a place to settle. "If it flies this way," thought Elena, "it will be a good omen." The sea-gull circled over one spot, folded its wings and, as though hit by a bullet, dropped out of sight with a plaintive wail, somewhere behind a dark ship. Elena shuddered and was ashamed of having done so, and without undressing she lay down on the bed by Insarov's side. He was breathing heavily and quickly.

# CHAPTER XXXIV

INSAROV WOKE UP late with a dull pain in his head, feeling, as he put it, horribly weak all over. He got up all the same.

"Hasn't Rendich been yet?" was his first question.

"Not yet," Elena replied, handing him the latest issue of *Osservatore Triestino*, in which there was much talk of war, of the Slav countries, and of the Principalities. Insarov began to read, while she started preparing his coffee. Somebody knocked at the door. "Rendich!" they both thought, but the man who knocked murmured in Russian, "Can I come in?"

Elena and Insarov exchanged astonished glances and, before they could reply, a dapper little man with a sharp little nose and alert little eyes walked into the room. He looked radiant, as if he had just won a fortune or had heard the most wonderful news.

Insarov rose in his chair.

"You don't recognize me," said the stranger, coming up to him in a jaunty manner and giving a polite bow to Elena, "Lupojarov, don't you remember, we met in Moscow at the E . . . . .'s?"

"Yes, at the E . . . . .'s," murmured Insarov.

"So it was, so it was! Will you introduce me to your wife? Madam, I've always had the greatest respect for Dmitri Vassilievich—(he corrected himself)—Nikanor

Vassilievich—and am very happy to have the honour of being introduced to you at last. Fancy,'' he continued, turning to Insarov, ''I only learnt last night that you were here. I'm also staying in this hotel. What a city, this Venice—a veritable poem. There's only one drawback— these horrible Austrians at every step! Oh, these Austrians, damn them! By the way, have you heard? There's been a decisive battle on the Danube—three hundred Turkish officers killed, Silistria* occupied. Serbia has already declared her independence. You, as a patriot, must be overjoyed! In me, too, all my Slav blood is roused. I'd advise you to be careful, though; I'm sure you're being followed. The spying here is terrible. Yesterday a sus- picious-looking character came up to me and asked, 'Are you a Russian?' I told him I came from Denmark. But you don't seem to be well, dear Nikanor Vassilievich, you must look after yourself. Madam, you must see that your husband gets well. Yesterday, I rushed about like a madman, looking at the palaces and churches—you've seen the Palace of the Doges, haven't you? What treasures there are everywhere! Particularly that great hall and the place left on the wall for the portrait of Marino Faliero† with the inscription '[Hic est Locus Marini Faletri] Decapitati pro Criminibus'. I've also been to see the famous prisons, and how my indignant spirit protested! You may remem- ber that I was always interested in social problems and was against the aristocracy—well, that's where I would put all supporters of the aristocracy—in those prisons. Byron was right when he wrote: 'I stood in Venice on the Bridge of

* Silistria: fortress of Roumania.—*Translator's note*.

† Marino Faliero, Doge of Venice, was executed for conspiracy 17 April, 1355.—*Translator's note*.

Sighs', though he, too, was an aristocrat. I was always for progressive ideas. The younger generation is all for progress. And what is your opinion of the English and the French? I wonder what they'll achieve, Boustrapas* and Palmerston. You know that Palmerston has become Prime Minister. No, say what you will, the Russian fist is no joke. What a rogue, that Boustrapas. Would you like me to lend you *Les Châtiments* by Victor Hugo—it's wonderful! 'L'avenir est le gendarme de Dieu!'—that's a daring phrase, but extremely powerful. Prince Viasemski was right, too, when he said: 'Europe keeps repeating Bash-Kadik-Lar, but keeps its eyes on Sinope.' I love poetry. I've also got Proudhon's latest book. There's nothing I haven't got. I don't know about you, but I'm glad about the war. I hope, though, that they won't call me back home, for I intend to go from here to Florence, then Rome. One can't go to France, so I think I'll go on to Spain—the women are wonderful there, they say, only too much poverty and too many insects. I'd like to make a dash to California—it's nothing for us Russians—but I promised an editor to make a detailed study of the question of trade in the Mediterranean. You may think it's not interesting, too specialized a problem, but we need specialists badly, we've had enough philosophizing. What we need now is something practical. But you do look ill, Nikanor Vassilievich. Perhaps I'm tiring you, but never mind, I'll stay a little longer. . . ."

And Lupojarov chattered away like this for a long time and when he went away promised to come back again soon.

* Boustrapas—denigrating nickname of Napoleon III.—*Translator's note.*

Exhausted by this unexpected visit, Insarov lay down on the sofa.

"Behold!" he said bitterly, with a glance at Elena, "your younger generation! Some of them may think themselves important and show off, but at heart they're just as hollow as this gentleman!"

Elena did not argue with her husband. At that moment she was much more preoccupied by Insarov's weakness than by the condition of the modern generation in Russia. . . .

She sat down by his side and took up her sewing. Pale and thin, he closed his eyes and lay still. Elena glanced at the sharp outline of his profile, at his emaciated hands, and a sudden fear caught at her heart.

"Dmitri . . ." she began.

He gave a start. "What? Has Rendich arrived?"

"Not yet . . . but what do you think about fetching a doctor . . . you're feverish, not really well at all. . . ."

"It's that chatterbox who has alarmed you. No. I'll have a short rest and it'll all pass. After dinner, we'll go out again . . . somewhere in the gondola."

Two hours passed. Insarov still lay on the sofa, but couldn't sleep, though his eyes were closed. Elena did not leave his side. Her sewing dropped on her lap and she sat motionless.

"Why don't you sleep?" she asked him at last.

"Just wait a moment." He took her hand and put it under his head. "Like that . . . that's lovely. You'll wake me as soon as Rendich comes, won't you? If he says that the ship is ready, we'll go at once. We must pack everything."

"It won't take long to pack," replied Elena.

"What a lot of nonsense that man talked about the war, about Serbia," Insarov murmured after a pause. "He probably made it all up. . . . But we must go, we must go. . . . We can't waste any more time. You must get ready."

He went to sleep and everything in the room was still.

Elena leant her head against the back of her chair and looked out of the window. The weather had changed for the worse. A wind had risen; large, white clouds raced across the sky and in the distance a slender mast was swaying, a long pennant with a red cross on it fluttered and fell, then fluttered again. The pendulum of an ancient clock ticked heavily, with a plaintive wheeze.

Elena closed her eyes. She had slept badly that night and gradually she, too, fell asleep.

She had a strange dream. She saw herself in a boat on the Tsaritsin lake with some strange people. They were silent and sat motionless; nobody was rowing, the boat moved of its own accord. Elena was not alarmed, but a little bored. She would have liked to know who these people were and why she was with them. She looked— and the lake grew wider, the banks disappeared—and it was not a lake any more, but an agitated sea; enormous blue waves silently and solemnly rocked the boat. Some rumbling, sinister thing was rising from the bottom of the sea; her unknown companions were jumping about, shouting and waving their hands. . . . Elena began to recognize their faces. Her father was among them. Then a whirlwind whipped up the waves—everything spun round and became blurred. Elena looked about her: everything was white and still, but now it was snow, snow, eternal snow. And she was not in a boat any more, but in a sleigh, as she was when she left Moscow. She was not alone; at her side was a small creature wrapped up in a shabby old cloak. Elena looked at her closely: it was Katia, her poor little friend. Elena was terrified. "Didn't she die?" she suddenly thought. "Katia, where are we going together?" Katia did not answer and wrapped herself more tightly in her cloak. She was cold. Elena was also shivering. She gazed down the long road. She could see a town through the powdery snow. Tall white towers with silver cupolas. . . . "Katia, Katia—is it Moscow?" No, thought Elena, it is the Solovetsk Monastery; there are many, many narrow little cells in it, like a beehive; it's hot and stuffy and Dmitri is locked up there. I must set him free. . . . Suddenly a grey, gaping abyss opened in front of her. The sleigh plunged into it. Katia laughed. "Elena! Elena!"—she could hear her calling down from the abyss. . . .

"Elena!" She heard her own name sounding clearly in her ears. She quickly raised her head, looked round and became numb. Insarov, white as snow, as the snow of her dream, had half-raised himself on the sofa and was looking at her with a bright and terrifying stare. His hair had fallen over his forehead, his lips were curiously parted. Terror, mixed with a kind of mournful beatitude, showed on his suddenly transfigured face.

"Elena!" he muttered, "I'm dying."

With a cry, she fell on her knees and pressed her head to his breast.

"This is the end," repeated Insarov, "I'm dying. . . . Good-bye, my poor darling! Good-bye my country!" And he fell back on the sofa. Elena ran out of the room, calling for help. The cameriere ran to fetch a doctor. Elena kept clinging to Insarov.

At that moment, a broad-shouldered, sunburnt man wearing a thick felt coat and a sou' wester appeared on the threshold. He stopped in surprise.

"Rendich!" exclaimed Elena, "You! Come here, look, for God's sake, what's the matter with him? He has fainted. Oh God! He went out yesterday, he was speaking to me a moment ago. . . ."

Rendich said nothing, only moved aside to make way for a little figure who hurried in, in a wig and wearing spectacles. It was the doctor who lived in the same hotel. He went up to Insarov.

"Signora," he said after a short pause, "il signor forestiere è morto . . . from an aneurism, complicated by disease of the lungs."

## CHAPTER XXXV

THE NEXT DAY, in the same room, Rendich was standing by the window. Elena sat in front of him, wrapped in a shawl. In the adjoining room Insarov lay in his coffin. Elena's face was both frightened and impassive; two lines had appeared on her forehead between her eyebrows and gave her motionless eyes a strained expression. On the window lay an opened letter from Anna Vassilievna. In it she begged her daughter to come to Moscow if only for a month, complained of her loneliness, of Nikolai Artemievich, asked after Insarov's health, sent him her greetings and asked him to allow his wife to come and see her.

Rendich was a Dalmatian, a seafaring man, with whom Insarov had made friends on his last trip to his country and whom he had found again in Venice. He was a rough, uncompromising, courageous man, devoted to the Slav cause. He despised the Turks, and hated the Austrians.

"How long must you stay in Venice?" Elena asked him in Italian. Her voice was just as lifeless as her face.

"One day to load without attracting suspicion—and then straight to Zara. Our compatriots won't like my news. They'd been waiting for him so long and had put all their hopes in him. . . ."

"They had put all their hopes in him," Elena repeated automatically.

"When is the funeral?" asked Rendich.

Elena did not answer at once. "To-morrow."

"To-morrow? I'll stay for it. I'd like to throw a handful of earth into his grave. And perhaps I can be of some help to you. But it would have been better for him to lie in a Slav grave."

Elena looked at Rendich. "Captain," she said, "take me and him along with you, to the other side, away from here. Can it be done?"

Rendich thought for a moment. "It can, but it'll be difficult. We'll have some trouble with the confounded authorities here. But assuming that we can fix all that and bury him at home—how am I to get you back?"

"You won't have to get me back."

"What do you mean? What will you do?"

"Leave that to me—only take us, take me."

Rendich scratched his head. "As you wish, but it'll all be very troublesome. I'll go and have a try. Wait for me here; I'll be back in about two hours."

He went away. Elena went into the next room, leant against the wall and stood like that for a long time, as though turned to stone. Then she sank down on her knees, but she could not pray. There was no reproach in her heart. She did not dare to ask God why He had not spared him, why He had not had pity on her and heard her prayer —why the punishment was greater than the sin deserved, if sin there had been. Each of us is guilty by the mere fact of being alive and even the great thinkers or benefactors of humanity cannot aspire to the right to live, to be spared on the strength of the good they do. Yet Elena could not pray; it was as if she had been turned to stone.

That night a large boat put off from the hotel where the Insarovs had stayed. In the boat were Elena and Rendich and a long box covered with a black cloth. They rowed for about an hour and at length reached a small two-masted ship which was riding at anchor at the very entrance of the harbour. Elena and Rendich went aboard and the sailors stowed the coffin. A storm broke out at midnight, but at dawn the ship had already passed the Lido. The storm reached a pitch of terrific violence during the day and experienced seafarers in the offices of Lloyd's shook their heads and expected the worst to happen. The Adriatic between Venice, Trieste and the Dalmatian coast is very dangerous.

About three weeks after Elena's departure from Venice, Anna Vassilievna received the following letter in Moscow:

My dearest Parents,

I am saying good-bye to you for ever. You will not see me again. Dmitri died yesterday. Everything, as far as I'm concerned, has come to an end. To-day I am leaving for Zara and taking his remains with me. I shall bury him there and what will happen to me then I don't know. But there is no other country for me any more, but the country of Dmitri. They are on the verge of revolution there and are preparing for war. I shall go as a nurse to the front and look after the sick and the wounded. I don't know what will happen to me, but I shall remain faithful to D's memory, to the cause that was his life—after his death. I have learnt to speak Bulgarian and Serbian. I shall probably not survive all this—if so, all the better. I have come to the edge of the abyss into which I must fall. Fate did not unite us in vain—who knows—maybe I was the cause of his death. Now it is his turn to take me with him. I looked for happiness and will perhaps find death. Probably it had to be so, probably—it was a sin. But death covers and reconciles everything, is that not so? Forgive me for all the grief I have brought to you—it was outside my control. As for returning to Russia—why should I? What should I do in Russia?

With my last kisses and blessings and hoping you won't misjudge me,

E.

Five years have gone by since that time and there has been no further news of Elena. All letters and enquiries have been fruitless. In vain did Nikolai Artemievich himself go to Venice, to Zara, after the conclusion of peace. In Venice he learnt only what the reader already knows, and in Zara nobody could give him any definite news about Rendich and the ship he had commandeered. There were dark rumours that a few years ago the sea, after a terrible storm, had cast adrift a coffin in which a man's body was found. Other, more reliable rumours, alleged that the coffin had not been cast adrift a all, but brought ashore and buried near the coast by a foreign lady who had come from Venice. Some people added that the lady was later seen in Herzegovina with the army, which had mustered there. They even described her clothes—black from head to toe.

At all events, every trace of Elena has vanished for ever, irrevocably; and nobody knows whether she is still alive or in hiding, or whether the petty business of her life is over, and over, too, it's brief paroxysm, and death in its turn has claimed her.

It happens that a man wakes up and asks himself with natural alarm: Am I really already thirty . . . forty . . . fifty years old? How is it that life has passed so quickly? How is it that death has approached so near? Death is like a fisherman who has caught fish in his net and leaves it for a time in the water; the fish can still swim, but the net surrounds them and the fisherman will pull it out in his good time.

What happened to the other characters in our story? Anna Vassilievna is still alive. . . . She has grown very old after the overwhelming blow; she complains less, but has become much sadder. Nikolai Artemievich has also aged and gone grey and has given up Augustina Khristianovna. . . . He now disparages everything foreign. His housekeeper, a handsome woman of about thirty, a Russian, struts about in silk dresses and wears gold rings and earrings. Kurnatovski, a man of passionate temperament and by virtue of his dark-haired virility a lover of pretty blondes, has married Zoë; she is completely under his thumb and has even given up thinking in German. Bersenev is in Heidelberg. He was sent abroad at Government expense—to Berlin and Paris. He makes good use of his time and will one day be an efficient professor. Two of his articles have attracted the attention of the learned public, *viz.*: *Some Peculiarities of Ancient German Law in Relation to Legal Punishment*, and *The Significance of Urbanization in Relation to Civilization*. A pity, though, that both articles are written in a ponderous style, with an abundance of foreign words.

Shubin is in Rome. He has devoted himself wholeheartedly to his art and is considered one of the most remarkable and promising of the younger sculptors. Critical visitors consider that he has not studied classical modes sufficiently, that he has no "style", and class him with the French school. He gets a great many commissions from England and America. Lately, one of his "Bacchantes" has given rise to a good deal of talk: the Russian Count Boboshkin, a well-known millionaire, was going to buy it for two hundred pounds, but preferred giving six hundred to another sculptor, a Frenchman *pur sang*, for a group representing "A Young Peasant-woman dying of Love on the Breast of the Spirit of Spring". Shubin corresponds occasionally with Uvar Ivanovich, the only one of them all who has not changed at all in any respect.

"Do you remember," he wrote to him recently, "what you said to me the night that poor Elena's marriage became known, when I was sitting on your bed talking to you? Do you remember, I asked you then whether we should ever have any real men, and you answered: "They'll come." Oh, black earth! Elemental soil! And now, from here, from my "beautiful retreat" I ask you once again— 'Well, Uvar Ivanovich, will they come?' "

Uvar Ivanovich twiddled his fingers and looked enigmatically into the distance.

**DATE DUE**